RIPPLES OF SILENCE

GERRY MAZER

JAE MAZER

FEATHERED
TENTACLE PRESS

For Dad. I love you.

Finish writing this book, or I will haunt you.

— GERRY MAZER, TO JAE MAZER

opper. And not just any copper, but warm, damp copper. Mark Ripley could smell it, feel it, thick and moist, hanging in the air. It hit him as soon as he opened the door of his '57 Ford Fairlane convertible. The lucky saps around him didn't have the pleasure of experiencing the onslaught of that metallic taste and smell. Not to the extent that he did.

Lucky bastards.

He walked softly padded softly onto the bland tile floor. The blues insisted on donning their precinct-issued heavy boots, but the vibration of them clopping around like obese Clydesdales was enough to rattle Ripley's brain clear out of his skull. He preferred the soft soles of his Topsiders, reverberating no more than a Q-tip tapping on carpet. The bustle of activity around him was a blur—

crime scene investigators and blues scattered every which way in his peripheral—but his senses honed to the smell and that acrid taste.

Death has been through here, living large as it passed.

A vibration, slight but detectable, rattled the hairs on the inside of his ear. He ignored it, pushing forward, not wanting to engage anyone just yet.

Bigger this time, his ears picking up the pulsating of a pair of syllables. That was good, he supposed. He had less of a surprise when a large hand wrapped around his shoulder and a bright white moon face obstructed his view.

"Ripley!" the face yelled.

"Yelling'll do you no good, you imbecile," Mark Ripley said, flicking Sutherland in the chest. "You can up the decibels, but you can't seem to crank up the smarts."

Sutherland huffed, scolding Mark with his eyes. *Punk,* Mark thought to himself. Didn't matter that the dick was pushing forty, he was still a spoiled little shit.

"Anyways," Mark said, "what's this all about?"

"Come see for yourself," Sutherland said, turning and leading the way into the building.

Dale Sutherland was the lead detective on this case. Sutherland had worked on the force for a lifetime, and had shared most of those with Mark in his vicinity, if not at his side. After the accident, and Mark's subsequent withdrawal from life, the two had fallen out of favour.

There was certainly no shortage of anger on either side, Mark blaming everyone for the state of the world that had left him less of a man, and Sutherland blaming Mark for, well, turning into a raging, gaping asshole. Regardless, Sutherland always turned to Mark when the going got tough, but it had to get real tough before his fingers texted that all too familiar number. *So what kind of shit show is this?* Mark wondered.

A veterinarian clinic, large and open, clean yet smelling of wet fur and the fear of canine and feline alike, with slight undertones of urine and vomit. It was the middle of the night, so the lobby was devoid of customers and their pets, but there was a bustle of activity, nonetheless. Police officer, beat cops and detective alongside crime scene investigators, were crammed into the lobby, behind the counter, and, presumably, in the backrooms. Despite the volume of working bodies, the room looked quiet; no lips were moving, no eyes were contacting. *This is something,* Mark thought. *This is something worse than usual.*

Sutherland led him through the double doors into the back hallway, and they passed by examination rooms on either side—six in total—each occupied by various precinct staff collecting evidence. They pushed through a second set of double doors into what looked like a recovery room; the walls lined with kennels and monitors. There was a window running along the entire back wall, providing a view of what looked like an operating room. There were monitors, surgical lights, medication carts, and a steel table in the center of the room. The far corner was cordoned off by black panel sheets erected to create a separate room for the crime scene itself. There was a red glow peeking out from around the curtains and reflecting onto the ceiling, quavering with a gentle movement. As Mark and Sutherland passed the window en route to the operating room, Mark noticed that the officers standing guard looked a peaked shade of green.

"Do I need to brace myself for this one?" Mark asked.

Sutherland stopped and turned, making sure to face Mark straight on for the delivery of this answer.

"There's no bracing yourself for this one, good buddy."

And in they went. Mark was almost knocked off his feet by the smell in the air. This was the epicenter; the point of origin of pain and blood and tissue that spread the stench of death all the way out to the open door of that '57 Ford convertible. Fortunately for his remaining senses, the fluorescent lights were off. Oh, how Mark hated fluorescent lights. They made his eyes buzz. But as he looked up, he realized they weren't off. They were gone.

"Don't think there was much going on here in the way of vet business," Sutherland said. "The bulbs are gone from all the sockets, including the hanging surgical lamp.

There's not even a goddamn flashlight in here. We brought in the floodlight so we could see what the hell we're doing. Not that we wanted to, mind you."

"Why are we here in the first place?" Mark asked. "Noise complaint?"

"Nope," Sutherland said. "Note."

"Note?"

Sutherland plucked an evidence bag off the table and handed it to Ripley. Ripley rubbed his eyes, struggling to make out the words in the dimly lit room.

> *The seeds of hate won't sow*
> *Here it begins*
> *Here I will go*
> *To never know*

THAT WAS IT. NO NAME, NOTHING MORE. MARK FLIPPED the letter over and found the address of the vet's office scrawled on the back. The writing, on both the poem and the address were written with a sharp point, tearing through the paper, this ink a dark brown.

Mark knew.

"It's blood, Mark," Sutherland said. "At first blush, it looks like it may have been penned with a quill. Difficult to be sure yet, but that's the assessment so far. Sicko fuck, this one."

"Because of his choice of writing utensil?"

"Well that," Sutherland said, combing his fingers through the thinning scuff of hair on the top of his head, "but more so this…"

Sutherland walked over to the black cloth blind shielding them from the corner of the room, tentatively pulled it aside, and barked something at the folks inside that made them drop what they were doing and haul outta their like their assess were on fire. They looked relieved to escape. Once the final staff had vacated the blocked off corner, Sutherland hooked back the blind, and tilted his head towards the great unknown.

"You coming in?" Mark asked.

"Not again," Sutherland said. "Not yet."

Mark stepped around Sutherland and entered the constructed crime scene lair. As the black curtain closed behind him, his senses narrowed, taking in one horrific detail at a time.

The smell. That coppery, wet stench. Fresh, metallic, mixed with an element of flora, likely mold or algae. The taste was the same—old, wet, sour. The air was cool. Mark's skin tingled a grimace as his eyes rolled over the scene.

A pod—a tube really—about three meters tall and a meter in diameter, was sitting in the corner of the room.

The pod was filled with liquid, thick and dark, a startling crimson. The entire corner of the room glowed red, the beam from the precinct's floodlight shining through the pod and reflecting it to all corners of the confined space. The liquid moved, rippling, creating a dance of blood shadows on the walls and ceiling. Although the liquid was dark, Mark could make out what was suspended within.

A man, only a few steps removed from being a boy, floated in the liquid, his arms bound over his head and his ankles to the ground, spread out like a starfish. His body swayed in motion with the minuscule swells, and every so often an arm or leg would float up against the glass. Mark caught a glimpse of some tearing on the man's wrists and ankles.

He fought. Of course he did. He was being tied down and submerged to his demise.

Mark questioned, however, if drowning was indeed the cause of death. The poor guy was suspended in liquid, sure, but the liquid was a deep crimson—blood, likely—and judging by the intense shade, it was more than just a drop. Mark stepped closer to the glass, trying to get a clearer look at the body through the sea of red, and got what he wanted. And what he didn't want.

The man was mutilated. Badly. Mark pressed his nose against the glass. He could make out a gory void where the guy's manhood used to hang, now just a vacant slab of ripped and cut flesh. His face seemed peaceful, unassuming and eerily calm; it was not the expression of someone fighting against the struggle of their lungs. Not that his face wasn't indicative of the horror though. His eyes, or rather where his eyes used to be, were vacant sockets, deep and bloody. But Mark knew that wasn't the final blow. The kill shot was likely the bone stabbed in one ear and protruding out the other; it was like his head was on a spit from ear to ear. It was unlikely that the bone was his, judging by the length and the fact that his limbs were intact. This bone came from someone or something else.

Mark felt unsettled. He had seen so much death in his career—much of it gory—but none as heinous as this. This was especially violent and calculated. This poor man was tortured. Mark looked around the room at the equipment, noting that the tube was hooked up to the water system adjacent to the surgical sink. Water was being recirculated by an external pump, causing the movement that wavered the light and floated the man's limbs. Beside the tank was a cart of tools ranging from medical to home improvement, none of them looking like they belonged in a veterinary office. There was a small flat screen television in the corner. It wasn't hooked up to any cable or satellite, and it wasn't a smart TV, but it was plugged into the wall, facing the line of sight of the victim.

How long did he keep you here?

Ripley breathed deeply through his mouth, overcome by the smell of death and the red light dominating his vision. He looked at the man, into his vacant sockets, and imagined his last moments.

Was he in the water before he died?

Did he think he was going to drown, or did the brain stab come first?

Did the removal of phallus and sight come before or after he expired?

Damn.

Mark closed his eyes and focused, imagining the sound of water in his ears like in a bathtub full of water. He let his body sway, picturing his own brown mop of curls floating above his head. He opened his eyes, once again studying the guy's face, hearing the bathtub water filling his ears, but now he was lost in that tube right alongside the doomed stranger.

"What d'ya make of this horse shit?" Sutherland said, approaching Mark from behind.

Of course Mark didn't respond. He hadn't seen Sutherland, so hadn't heard him. He just stayed face to face with the blind and deaf corpse floating in the water before him, hoping that the corpse's lips would start moving to tell him the ending to this story.

DAYLIGHT HOURS CLAWED THEIR SPRITELY FINGERS OVER the horizon, pouring over the world. The added light didn't help lift any moods at the crime scene though. It made clearer the darkness of the night before. Evidence had been collected, photographs had been taken, and the coroner was wheeling the body off to load into her van. Ripley stood, back against the tree line, observing the scene from afar, trying to make a holistic assessment before some dumbass came to distract him.

The veterinary clinic was nestled in beside a string of businesses—a dentist, a nail salon, and a farm supply store. The businesses were protected enough by the trees, and far enough from the main road, that no one would notice tomfoolery unless they came off the main road in search of it; it was tucked in the back of an average lot, shaded by the overhang of seasoned poplars and willows. There a good distance between the vet clinic and the other three businesses—good for keeping the peace when customers are the barking, howling kind.

Or screaming and dying.

"Sutherland!" Ripley yelled out. Sutherland was speaking to the day shift, briefing them and assigning tasks to work on while he took his authority back to the precinct to conduct the orchestra from afar. Upon hearing Ripley's summon, Sutherland waved off the detectives and made a beeline across the parking lot.

Ripley knew he had been stand-offish with Sutherland, so any initiation of communication was eagerly welcomed.

"Thoughts, old friend?" Sutherland asked.

"Dunno yet," Ripley answered. "Surveillance?"

"Nope. There were cameras, but they must have been removed whenever the suspect took up residence."

"Witnesses?"

"None. Like I said, no one had a clue anything was amiss. If it wasn't for that note…"

"Prints?"

"Hundreds, of course. This was a fairly busy veterinary clinic before they went out of business, judging by the reviews on Yelp. We're gonna try to track down the most recent appointment, see how long the place has been out of commission."

Ripley sighed.

"I assume you'll canvas the friends and customers of all the businesses, see if you can dig up any dirt. See if they can recall any unusual traffic."

Sutherland shifted uncomfortably from foot to foot, looking at the ants weaving around his boots.

"Oh please," Ripley said. "You can't still be squeamish."

"Damn it, Ripley," Sutherland said. "It's like you try to make people uncomfortable."

Ripley was going to snap a retort, but he knew what

Sutherland said was true. Since his accident, Ripley's weapon against the shame of his injuries was to make others ashamed and uncomfortable; it was better to deflect the attention from him to their own inability to address their social discomfort. But being a dick was counterproductive.

"Sorry, Dale," Ripley said, now looking down at his own trail of ants. "It still eats at me, you know?"

"I know, buddy," Sutherland said, clapping Ripley on the back. "We are all here for you, if you ever want to come back to the force. There are ways to accommodate—"

"I think the time away has been therapeutic," Ripley interrupted, staving off an awkward conversation. "Besides, the money as a private consultant is just what the doctor ordered."

They stood in silence for a moment, both having so much to say but nothing that could be put into words.

"Anyhow," Ripley said, "I'd like to buzz down to the station after you get everything catalogued and organized, take a boo at the evidence and see if I can at least put together the edge pieces of this puzzle."

"Good plan," Sutherland said. "Give us a day or so, let us get some searching and interviews done so we have something to put in front of you. Go get some rest. It's been a long night."

It had. A long night, and an exhausting decade.

Ripley smiled and headed towards his car, knowing that behind those pained smiles and clumsy waves was gossip full of pity and sadness; declarations of personal and professional doubts and slanders were being uttered behind notepads and hands blocking lips that he was forbidden to read. The explosion may have stolen his hearing, but it heightened his ability to read people and the surrounding environment.

As Ripley dropped down into the sunken seat of his car, he sat for a moment, picturing the solace of his couch, the comfort of a big greasy pizza loaded with bacon, and the distraction of another subtitled, sci-fi flick that relied more on CGI and expressions than sound effects. But until then, he would have to endure the long drive home on the cluttered freeway, a drive that used to be a great opportunity to debrief after a particularly grueling shift. He never thought he'd see the day he would long for the benign, sterile chatter of those idiots on the radio station; anything to help his mind stray from the image of that young man in the tube. As he pulled out of the gravel parking lot, he could still see that red glow from the liquid lingering in his eyes, and hear water rippling in his ears.

CHAPTER 2

Ripley slammed into his house, trying to hold back the guck that had been rising into his throat on the way home. The more he thought about the grizzly crime scene, the worse he felt. Throwing his keys on the side table by the door, he stormed to the bathroom and dropped to his knees in front of the toilet. He tried to throw up, but all he got was dry heaving—stinging, foul tasting bile. Grabbing a glass by the sink, he rinsed out his mouth three times then stared at his reflection in the mirror. "What kind of fuckin' sick bastard could do that?" he growled at his image.

Ripley clasped the sides of the sink and willed his body to settle down. He'd seen plenty of messy murder scenes over his time with the PD, but never like this one.

He stared at his reflection while scenes from the bizarre murder flashed though his brain like tumbling, gory playing cards. Each imagined scene brought another lurch to his already beleaguered digestive system.

Finally, he was able to calm down. Driving his thoughts off the murder, he studied his forever changed face. A permanent scar, like a white bolt of lightning, shot across his face from over his left eyebrow, across the top of his nose, and down his right cheek. Because of his six foot, five inch height, he had to stoop down below the top of the mirror a little to to examine the slash. It had been almost two years since the explosion. This scar was permanent. He supposed that a specialist could reduce it a little, but he had become accustomed to it, and wore it like a morbid medal of honour.

Ripley's dark hair, piercing ice-blue eyes, and angular face would have been very attractive if it hadn't been for the scar. Freshly passed forty but could easily pull off twenty, he often passed for one of his son's friends rather than his father. *Oh well,* he mused, as he turned away and headed wearily to the bedroom to get some much-needed shut eye.

As he climbed into bed, his thoughts drifted back to that fateful explosion. At the time he was the lead detective at a crime scene in the Beverly neighbourhood, a seedy, crime ridden area of the city. Entering the abandoned office along with other members of the PD, he was unaware that a hidden bomb was about to explode. He had been focused on the body propped up on a chair in the middle of the room. Blood drenched the victim's face and the front of his hairy, shirtless chest and stomach, and pooled, on the concrete floor. It appeared that his abdomen had been slashed open, then crudely sewn up. Puzzled, Ripley had leaned closer...

The next thing he knew, he was waking up in the hospital, bandages everywhere, numb with pain, and totally deaf. His wife, Sarah, was weeping profusely; his sidekick from work, Dale Sutherland, had his hand on her shoulder; and his son, Tommy, was in the background, devastated more than the rest of them combined. "Where in Hell am I?" Ripley had croaked, trying to sit up. A nurse by his side that he hadn't noticed before put her hand on his shoulder and gently pushed him back down. "You're in Saint Gabriel's Hospital," she said. "There was an explosion." He didn't hear a word. His head had a constant ringing in it that was driving him crazy, but he understood where he was and that he was hurt, so he reluctantly settled back.

Sarah approached cautiously, like he was contagious or something, and started yammering at him and crying at the same time. Ripley just stared helplessly at her through bandages covering most of his face while Sutherland gently took her arm and coaxed her back to her chair. Tommy turned his face away, the sheen of moisture on his cheeks shining in the light.

Later that day, after everyone except Dale Sutherland had left, a doctor entered and carefully examined Mark's wounds. The nurse wrote the doctor's comments on a pad which she shared with Ripley as the doctor spoke. "Your lower body injuries are minor and will heal quickly, but your hearing may be permanently damaged. And you're going to have quite a scar across your face. You're lucky your eyes weren't damaged. I will have a specialist examine you to see if there is any possibility that your hearing can be saved. In the meantime, get some rest."

That night, as a doped up Ripley stared groggily at the ceiling, depression began to drop over him like a black, heavy, stifling mist. *My life is over,* he groaned. *The PD will toss me aside like a sack of potatoes.*

Part of his prediction came true. The force sidelined him to a permanent desk job pushing paper. Anger and depression led him to quit in disgust. He barred himself in his bedroom for most of the day every day, wallowing in a flood of self pity. Sarah had trouble dealing with this new reality and started avoiding him like the plague. His son, Tommy, was the only one who stayed by his side. Gradually, Tommy helped him to emerge from his melancholy and begin to look forward to a new life without sound.

Ripley's spirits lifted day by day, and Churchill's

famous words rang through his mind: "Never give up! Never, never give up!" Ripley was ready to move on.

Ripley attacked his new reality with a vengeance. He studied sign language and lip reading, sometimes up to twelve hours a day. Tommy worked with him constantly until his proficiency was solid. Ripley decided that if he couldn't be on the force, he'd do the next best thing and set himself up as a private consultant. This lead to him becoming a consultant for the PD on the more serious murder cases. Captain Sloan, his old boss, wasn't happy about Ripley being sidelined by the Chief. He considered Ripley to be one of the best lead detectives he ever had, so it wasn't much of a leap to bring him back as a consultant, and it had already paid off on two cases. The harder the case, the more complex the perp, the more Ripley shone.

Ripley was back on track with work, but his new reality with Sarah took a bitter change in direction. It appeared that, when it came right down to it, she was in love with the uniform and not the man. His hearing loss and scar didn't help. Quitting his job with the force was the final straw, and she forced him to move out. The divorce followed quickly on some trumped up grounds. About the only thing he had left was weekly visits with Tommy, and his '57 Ford Fairlane Skyliner convertible. He loved both Tommy and his Skyliner. In that order, of course.

~

RIPLEY WOKE WITH A START. THE BIZARRE MURDER SCENE had played like a bad movie through his mind all night, resulting in a fitful sleep. After his morning absolutions, he walked over to the window with his morning coffee and gazed fondly at his car. It seemed silly to love an old car, but he couldn't help himself. There was a bit of his father in the that old relic, and he had loved his pop dearly. It saddened Ripley. His eyes misted over, and he thought of the terrible car accident that killed both his mother and father just before the explosion. The explosion and his parent's demise were a double whammy in his life which was then crowned off by Sarah's abandonment.

His eyes cleared, and he gazed at the second love of his life. The swooping chrome lined fins; the two toned gold and white interior and the dazzling gold and chrome slash down the side along with the powerful Thunderbird engine, made this one of the greatest classics ever. It wasn't in perfect condition, but almost. One of the unique features of the Skyliner was the retractable hard top that would slide in and out of the trunk at the push of a button. Ripley loved that. He planned to keep it and keep improving it until it was in perfect showroom condition. And when he got too old to drive, it would go to Tommy.

Time to get to the precinct and focus on the bizarre

murder case at hand. Ripley grabbed his well-worn jeans, a clean, button down white shirt, and brown suede walking shoes. Soon he was grooving down the freeway with the top down, focused on details of the gruesome scene. Why did the murderer send them a poem written in blood with the address of the crime scene written on the back? Why was the victim mutilated in such a horrendous fashion? What about the bone through the head from ear to ear? Where did that come from?

Suddenly, Ripley remembered something unusual from the crime scene. He knew that his sense of smell had been vastly heightened since he lost his hearing. It was like some sort of cruel compensation. At the crime scene he had smelled the coppery, wet odour of blood along with many other odours that usually accompanied vet clinics, but he did smell something else that was different and yet familiar. The recognition of the smell eluded him, but he knew he had smelled it before. He puzzled about this as he spun the Skyliner into the precinct parking lot and climbed the concrete steps into his former place of employment.

Blues everywhere. Every direction he turned, more blues. He knew most of them. Many had become accustomed to his injuries, but some still whispered behind their hands, eyes cast in his direction. A big paw grabbed his shoulder. He spun around, expecting to see Sutherland taunting him, but it was Captain Sloan, big, wide, and bald.

"Good to see you back in action, Ripley," Sloan said, smiling through coffee-stained teeth. "Some of my guys called in sick after seeing the mess yesterday. Don't blame 'em." He turned suddenly serious. "Let's go to my office. Sutherland," he barked off to the side, "you too." Dale Sutherland, who was hovering nearby, followed them to the Captain's inner chambers while all the blues stared at them, no doubt wondering what was next.

"Sit," Sloan ordered. "New developments." Ripley and Sutherland obediently sat on the oak wooden chairs facing the Captain's messy, piled-high oak desk. "Close the damn door," Sloan said, glaring at Sutherland.

After Sutherland returned to his chair, Captain Sloan grabbed a glass container with his meaty paw and passed it to Ripley. "Got another fuckin' poem," he said quietly. "This one was inside the victim's body, glass container and all."

Ripley and Sutherland stared at the container with the wrinkled note inside. It was small and tubular, about the dimensions of a large pill container. It was clear glass with a black sealed cap, like a specimen container from a lab. It had been cleaned down in the morgue, but there were remnants of tissue in the small crevices of the serrated cap. The poem inside was written on a piece of paper taped face out against the glass, and appeared to be written in blood, similar to the first one. It looked like the same writing as the first note, too.

THE SEEDS OF HATE
No more will sow
So much better
To never know

"WHAT THE FUCK?" SUTHERLAND SAID. "MAKES NO SENSE. Gobbledegook."

"It's got to mean something," Captain Sloan interjected. "Put it with the first one and see if the two together make sense." He pulled the first note from the evidence file. "We analyzed the blood from both notes. Same blood. It's not from not the victim, but they are both from the same donor. Human."

He placed both poems side by side:

THE SEEDS OF HATE A FAILED ATTEMPT
No more will sow But here you go
So much better You get the idea
To never know I'll make it so

RIPLEY AND SUTHERLAND stared at both notes, completely baffled. "It means absolutely nothing to me," Sutherland said. "Seems like blathering bullshit. My head hurts thinking about this."

Ripley grinned. "That's because your head is full of shit!"

Sutherland punched him in the arm and got up. "Let's go see the coroner, asshole. She may be ready to review what she found during the autopsy."

CHAPTER 3

He carefully opened the three buttons of his meticulously ironed polo shirt, then, rather than pulling it over his head, he grasped the fabric on either side and ripped it from his body. He took the mangled fabric, wiped the blood from his face, and tossed it towards the rubbish bin underneath the desk. He missed. Unleashing a string of expletives, he crossed the room and kicked the all-inanimate shit out of that garbage can.

"Trashy fucker," he spat at the now splintered plastic receptacle. "Could anything else fuck me today?

The contents of the room remained silent, from the furniture to the books, the portable floodlights, and the decommissioned dental chair in the center of the room.

The silence was stifling, and he became aware of the raspiness of his own breathing.

"Yes. Some television would be nice."

He pulled off his latex gloves and grabbed the television remote out of the makeshift cup holder he had affixed to the side of the dental chair. Pointing it at the moderately sized television in the corner, he pressed the power button and dropped the remote back into the cup holder without bothering to check what programming would appear.

"Better not be the goddamn news. Bullshit. Piles of it."

He didn't know what he had turned on, nor did it stifle the silence ringing in his ears. The volume was off, as it always was, and he had already rotated his chair so that his back faced the screen. He wanted to feel like there was something lively in the room with him, but had no time to acknowledge it. He reached over and pulled out another set of gloves. He stretched them on his hands with a scowl on his face, cursing the sheath that blocked his skin from the satisfaction of physical contact; he did enjoy the intensity of skin on skin.

"Must be done. Must be done. Nosy Nellies here and there. Nosy Nellies everywhere."

After the gloves were finally in place, he used his forearm to wipe the sweat from his forehead, then rolled his stainless steel stool up to the dentist's chair. He closed his pale eyes and reached his hand out, groping clumsily until his fingers met the meaty flesh of a warm thigh. He stopped, flattening his palm against the firm quad muscle, longing to feel the tender skin against his own. Flesh was so beautiful, so innocent, so benign. He leaned so close that the stubble on his sharp jaw-line grazed the flesh on the inside of the thigh. He froze, calculating just how much of that skin had come in contact with his.

"Clumsy."

He opened his eyes and looked at the thigh, then shrugged.

"Well, maybe go all in now, right?"

He took the gloves off, closed his eyes, and wrapped his bare hands around the thigh. He kneaded and squeezed, caressed and tickled. He loved the feeling of the give, the cellulite, the goosebumps. After several minutes of tactile indulgence, he shuddered and rolled his stool away from the chair.

"So worth it."

Rolling the gloves inside out, he tucked them in the pocket of his overpriced jeans, then undid his belt. Leisurely, he stripped down to nothing, neatly folded his clothes, and walked to the door. After unlocking a series of deadbolts and chains, he entered a dark hallway. When the solid door closed behind him, he was bathed in complete darkness. He drew a breath, and felt himself grow hard at the nothingness that enveloped him. He walked along the dirt floor, his footfalls barely a whisper, until he reached the other end of the hall. He glanced up the stairs, leading to a ceiling hatch, but chose the room on the left. He sighed as he pressed the handle and pushed the door open, allowing a flickering light to breach the visual serenity of the black hallway. He walked into the room with conviction, clothes tucked under his arm and finger pointing accusingly.

"Fuck you!" he said, his finger wagging at a large wood stove burning brightly in the center of the otherwise empty room.

He stood still for a moment, finger extended, locked in a stare-down with the old wood stove. Then he laughed.

"Naw. You're nothing. You got a job to do, and that's that."

He reached out, cranked the handle, and opened the door, allowing tendrils of flame to lick out at his naked body.

"Too bad you couldn't reach into the hall. It's a mite chilly out there. But then, you'd bring more light, so..."

He trailed off, lost in his own internal dialogue. Shifting the clothes to his hands, he tossed them one by one into the intense inferno. The fire warmed him straight to the bone, and he closed his eyes for a moment, allowing himself to enjoy the flames casting dancing shadows against the lids of his eyes. He hummed an opera reverberating in his brain, then snapped his fingers.

"Rossini. That's who should be playing. I haven't heard him in the longest time."

With that, he spun on his heels and left the room. After a brief but grounding journey through the black hallway, he was back in the room, attending to a small record player in the corner that came to life with the sounds of Seville. He sat on his stool, pulled a steel cart towards him, and a plethora of tools clanked and clattered as the wheels traversed the earthy floor. His fingers hovered over the gleaming blades and hooks and pliers, finally descending upon a very fine, thin blade with a slight curve; it looked like a miniature scythe. He lifted it to the light, admiring it, then held it out in front of a pair of wet, brown eyes.

"Isn't it lovely? I made it myself. I make *all* of them myself. They're well crafted, unique, beautiful. You'll love it. You'll see. Well, you won't *see*..."

He broke into raucous laughter, a throaty bray that echoed through the room despite the dirt floors and padded walls. The brown eyes twitched frantically, tears overflowing and rolling down ashen cheeks.

"No? You don't see the humour in it? Oh well. Fuck

you, then. At least you'll appreciate it when this is all done."

His foot searched the floor until it found a pedal. He stepped on it, slowly lowering the head of the dentist's chair until the brown eyes were looking up at him. He adjusted the head slightly, turning it towards him so he could look at it square-on, then placed his hand tenderly on a cheek. He moved the face from side to side, sizing it up, then leaned close enough that he could smell the sour fear on its breath. He shuddered as he felt himself get hard again; his firmness, uninhibited by clothing, pressed against a stray arm swinging off the side of the chair.

"Don't get frisky with me. I'm not interested in that. That being said, this is rather scintillating, isn't it? We'll see if I finish before *he* does."

He winked down at his erect member, smirking at his own wit. He gave his head a shake to compose himself, then leaned in again, this time steadying his arm on the head of the chair. He moved close, so close, until the sides of their noses were pressed together. With the tips of his fingers, he held the eyelids open as wide as he could, capillaries shooting through the already bloodshot sclera. He released a sniper's exhale, then pressed the sharp tool into the edge of the iris. The brown eyes screamed.

~

IT WAS A CAREFUL AND DRAWN-OUT PROCESS, AN HOUR IN all. The brown eyes had been removed, carefully sliced away, leaving the sockets bloody but cleanly sliced. His leg and the stray arm were sticky with warm semen, a release he simply couldn't contain at the moment his blade penetrated the second eye.

"That was amazing. Was it as good for you as it was for me?"

He didn't wait for an answer. There wouldn't be one, of course.

"Now don't think me a monster. It's not your *pain* I enjoy. It's your future. Your outcome. *Our* outcome."

He stood, allowing his completion to trickle down his leg and into the dirt, and walked over to the counter where he had a glass jar set out on the counter. He brought the eyes up to his lips, gave them an air-kiss, then plopped them into the jar. After filling it with formaldehyde, he secured the lid in place and set the jar in a cupboard overtop the counter. He closed his eyes, inhaled deeply, then became acutely aware of his environment. The stickiness of his skin, the smell of blood in the air, the stink of fear and sweat and bleach.

His blood boiled, throwing him into a convulsive rage. He lunged at the surgical cart beside the chair, throwing it across the room with a deafening clank. The noise caused him to drop to his knees, and the feeling of wet earth grinding into his skin made him dry heave. He quickly stood and made a feeble attempt to wipe off the dirt, instead smearing it together with the already wet patch on his inner thigh.

"Fuck!"

He wheeled over a pail he had rigged up on a trolley and retrieved the sieve hanging from an IV pole attached to the side. He flipped a lever and liquid poured out. He proceeded to douse himself and his patient with the fluid. He scrubbed his own flesh until his legs were raw and bloodied, and chaffed the stray arm until it was stripped clean, almost to the bone. The smell of bleach burned the inside of his nostrils, and his eyes poured like a faucet, distorting his vision.

He shut down the bleach pump, wheeled the rig back to the corner, and fetched a sheet of plastic from one of the cupboards. He went into the black hallway, spread the sheet out on the floor, and laid down on it, snuggling in and wrapping himself like a cocooned insect. He saw nothing. He felt the plastic crinkling here and there over his nakedness, and all he heard were the crinkles of the sheet each time he drew breath. It was cathartic. Once his heart slowed and his rage was hidden, he unravelled himself and picked up the plastic. After depositing it into the wood stove in the room at the end of the hall, he returned to his work.

"Sorry about that. My reactions are unbecoming, I

know. I'm usually more in control, but I like a clear head when I'm down here, doing my work. Medication that calms me muddies me as well. Nevertheless, that kind of savage behaviour needs to stop. I apologize. It won't happen again—to me, to anyone. Now let's get you ready to go."

He went to work on a wooden crate in the corner of the room, lining it with plastic sheeting, hay, and confetti. Once the inside was fashioned into a cozy nest, he went over to the dentist's chair and heaved up his limp cargo.

"Dead weight, aren't you?"

He released another belly-deep chortle, then stumbled. The stray arm brushed against his lower abdomen. He dropped the patient, who landed with a heavy thud on the floor.

The rage came back with a brief vengeance. Drooling and sputtering, he brandished a machete hung from a nearby hook on the wall and removed the patient's offending limb. Once the detached groper had been tossed to the side, his calm returned. He brushed himself off, then hoisted the dead weight up once more, this time without interference. He placed the patient back in the chair long enough to cauterize the amputation with a torch, then hauled it over to its intended destination. Once the cargo was nestled comfortably in the crate, he wheeled over an IV pole and oxygen tank. He hooked them up tenderly, taking care to use a butterfly needle on the IV and a high-quality mask for the oxygen.

"For your comfort, of course. You've been through enough already."

Eighty-two nails later, the crate was sealed and propped on a dolly, ready for delivery. He set it in the corner out of the way until the rest of his work was complete. He needed the place ready and waiting for his next creation to begin. He wiped down the dentist chair with the bleach solution, polished the counters, disposed of all his handmade tools, and wiped down every surface one, two, three times. He wasn't all that worried about evidence—the cops were too damn stupid and ignorant to figure out they should come for a visit. He was simply concerned about cross contamination. He needed his projects free and clear of interference. A clean slate was important. So important.

Standing back, he perused the room, inspecting his own toils. It looked pristine and smelled of nothing but dirt wet with bleach. He would crank open the vent when they left, rid the place of the staleness and chemical assault that turned his excitement to tears. He was about to call it good when a movement of color and light caught his eye.

The fucking television.

Despite loathing the media, he had turned it on as a

distraction, then got distracted back to his work. He laughed to himself once again, and walked over to the set, fingers reaching for the power button.

He stopped.

The screen. The scene. Judging by the pink light hovering low in the sky, the footage was from the wee hours of the morning. The trees blew gently in the wind, silent witnesses to creation and birth, life and death. Hordes of the ignorant were milling about, chatting nonchalantly, picky-picking here and there, this and that, things of little importance.

He dropped to his knees, grasping the television on either side, mesmerized by the progression of his story.

"As long as you don't interfere. Read the message, just don't cowrite the book."

People moved about as he expected they would, then the gurney appeared, wheeled out the front door of the veterinarian clinic by a stunning coroner. A heavily-painted news reporter spewed some bullshit, hair sprayed stiff to combat the breeze, no doubt embellishing details she did not yet possess, all for the sake of shock and awe and advertising dollars. The pigs milling about looked morose and fretful—overwhelming and apathetically disgusted.

"You are horrified, but at the wrong thing, you rancid bitches."

He was about to turn away from the set, unimpressed

by the stereotypical setting and reactions before him, but a glimmer of possibility caught his eye. An unexpected surprise. He cocked his head and focused in on a nearly stationary figure on the corner of the screen. A man, probably in his forties, stood by the tree line, his body moving with the breeze. It appeared he was taking in his surroundings—looking around, assessing, feeling everything. This man watched everything carefully, breathing deeply, and winced at what appeared to be a foul smell.

He watched the man on the television, mesmerized by his movements, his odd affect, his reactions to the surrounding action. The coroner slammed the door to the van, and everyone on the screen jumped like ants on a trampoline. The man turned his head to look; he knew the door had been shut, but hadn't startled at it. He had *felt* it.

"Well now..."

He shuffled on his knees over to the dentist's chair, fumbled in the cupholder for the remote, and returned to the television, pausing the picture while the man was still by the trees. He was now facing another man.

Well, hello, Mr. Sutherland.

The man and Sutherland were having what looked to be a mundane professional conversation, no doubt regarding the crime scene. He lifted his pinky finger, touching it to the screen where the man's face was, and stoked his tiny cheek.

"Hello there, new friend."

He watched as the man studied Sutherland's face every time Sutherland uttered a word. The man listened, but he did not hear.

"Well, well, well. Who are we?"

Ripley and Sutherland thrust themselves through the swinging doors of the morgue.

"Hey Mark," Jackie Fields looked at Mark, lingering on his face for a moment before addressing Sutherland. "Dale."

Fields was standing overtop a stainless steel exam table. "About time you showed up. We have some interesting developments here."

She discarded her blood-coated latex gloves and signaled the men over to the table. The antiseptic odour mixed with the coppery smell of blood was almost overwhelming to Ripley's hyper-sensitive olfactory system. Once again, Ripley's brows crinkled as he smelled the faint scent of something else; it was the same smell as the murder scene, familiar but not quite identifiable. He drew his attention back to Fields.

Dr. Fields seemed too young to be in the position of Chief Coroner. Most of the doctors Mark had encountered over the years were old, crusty, and male. Aside from the fact that she was young and strikingly beautiful, Jackie Fields' reputation over recent years had quickly ascended to the point where she was one of the best in the city. In fact, she was well-renowned province wide. Standing over the table in her stark white lab coat, which she somehow kept spotless amid the fluids and gore, she looked like an angel with her long black hair and striking green eyes. Mark didn't know her age, but he assumed she was somewhere in her thirties. She reminded him of Morena Baccarin, an actress who played a coroner in the TV series, Gotham. He could barely take his eyes off her.

Sliding her long, slender hands into a new pair of gloves, she looked him in the eye with a crooked smirk on her face, causing his heart to skip a beat.

"Focus, Ripley. Eyes on the subject," she said, pointing down at the corpse on the slab. "My autopsy is complete on John Doe here, but besides the obvious trauma to the body, nothing unusual has shown up anywhere, including the blood analysis. The only real items of interest are the note I removed from the stomach—which I believe the victim was forced to swallow, tube and all, before he was killed—and this bone."

She picked up a slender, thirty-centimeter long bone from a steel tray. It was the bone that had been rammed clear through the victim from ear to ear. The blood and brain tissue were washed off, and one end was sharpened, making it easier to pierce through the young man's head.

"This bone fragment is curious for two reasons," she continued. "First is that it is human, but not from this young man. It appears to be skeletal remains from someone long ago expired; thirty years or more by my calculations. Second, it appears the perp left a message using some sort of carving tool." Slowly, she turned the bone over in her delicate fingers. She pointed to a spot near the blunt end. Carved distinctly into the bone were two letters : A and S. "Obviously the perp spent some time making sure these letters were clear and prominent so we wouldn't miss them. I have no idea what they mean." She picked up a magnified image she had taken of the carved bone and handed it to Ripley.

They all stared intently at the meticulously carved letters. "A-S," Ripley said under his breath. "Maybe it's the initials of the perp? Like Andrew Smith or something. Brainy idea for someone who doesn't want to be caught."

"That can't be it. Too easy," Sutherland mused, staring at the deeply engraved letters.

"But they're there for a purpose," Ripley said. "He or

she is trying to tell us something. We need to work on finding all possibilities."

Sutherland sneered. "Can't be a woman. What female would be strong enough to maneuver a body like this?" He furrowed his bushy eyebrows as he glared at the photo. "Some dick with a grudge. A random asshole. AS… ass. Let's call him the ass. He grinned at Ripley and Fields, but got only disgusted frowns in response.

Ripley returned his attention to Dr. Fields. "Captain Sloan told us the blood on the note was human, but it wasn't the victim's. Anything there?"

"They only thing we found was that the blood was fresh, a few days at most. And it's a rare blood type—AB negative. This category of blood is so rare that it's only found in about one percent of the population. The victim's blood is type O, RH positive, which is very common."

"Thanks, Doc," Ripley said, smiling at Jackie. "Let us know if anything else pops up." He looked at Sutherland. "Let's go, shit head. We've got work to do. Murder doesn't solve itself."

CHAPTER 5

When they returned to the station, they strode through the blue herd and headed for the conference room. Ripley, being a consultant, did not have an office or a desk, so the conference room had become operational headquarters. Facing Sutherland across the long, oak table, Ripley said, "We need to divvy up the work. You start researching the rare blood type to see if possible candidates can be narrowed down and identified, and I'll play with those letters we saw."

"Sounds boring, and I know it won't lead anywhere," Sutherland retorted, "but I'll surf the system and see what I can find. Have fun trying to figure The Ass out." He scowled as he got up and slammed the door on the way to his desk.

Ripley sighed. Through the door, he could hear Sutherland talking up a storm with the blues about 'The Ass'. He thought this was a huge joke.

Sometimes that guy can be a real pain.

The longer he knew Dale Sutherland, the less he liked him. Unfortunately, due to captain's orders, he had to work with him. The Sloan had been pairing the two together ever since Ripley had returned as a consultant. They'd worked well together in the old days when Ripley was still on the force back when Sutherland was more likable and focused on doing a good job.

Good thing Sloan lets me take the lead on these cases. I couldn't work under Sutherland.

For a moment, Mark's thoughts drifted to Jackie Fields. She was single, smart, and beautiful, but the mess from his first marriage made him hesitant to move forward. His former wife, Sarah, was difficult to live with most of the time, and when she became pregnant, she drifted away even further. When he did see her, she was distant or argumentative, seemingly without reason.

At the time of Tommy's birth, Ripley was away on a mandatory training course and had asked Sutherland—his then friend and fellow officer—to be there for Sarah if he couldn't get home in time. Sutherland was glad to comply. When Mark got home a few days after the birth, he saw his amazing son, Tommy, for the first time. And his angry wife. Somehow the whole mess was his fault, and she was going to make him pay. Things were unbearably strained for some time after that, but it eventually settled down to a dull roar and life carried on. Until the explosion. Now he was alone, but not quite ready to move on.

An hour later, Ripley was staring at the letters on the bone. He had come up with some possible ideas, but none of them made sense. Just as he was about to sift through Fields' medical report, the door slammed open and Sutherland barged in like the proverbial bull in a china shop. "Okay, Silent Sam," he sneered, looking at the mostly empty pad Ripley was scribbling on. "I've done my job, and I see you're just sitting there with your finger up your ass like always."

Ripley knew what Sutherland said, but pretended he hadn't been looking at him when he said it. "Say again? You have to let me see your fat lips or you're just blowing smoke." Sutherland knew he was being played, so he just ignored the question and sprawled in the chair opposite Ripley. "I'm not making much headway," Ripley sighed, deflating the bravado that might incite battle. "How about you?"

"Like I said, I've done my job," Sutherland said. "We're scanning the system for matches to the blood type in the notes, and the paper type, sellers, all that."

Work other people are doing for *you.*

The door opened and Captain Sloan popped his

gigantic bald head through. "Looks like we got another one, guys," he said, the stress evident in his eyes.

"Another what?" Ripley asked, taking note of the severity in the captain's tone.

"We got another note in blood, and an address on the back."

"What?" Sutherland said, finally looking serious.

"A note, goddamnit," Captain Sloan growled, "dropped off at reception with the rest of the mail. Same as before. Get on it. Now! I want you guys there first before any possible contamination occurs. CSI will be right behind you."

ROARING DOWN THE BOULEVARD IN SUTHERLAND'S BLACK and white with the sirens blaring, they reached the crime scene within ten minutes. It was an abandoned warehouse next to the rail line in a drab area framed by grey, blank-faced buildings. They gained access through an unlocked entrance next to a huge overhead door. In weak, dusty light seeping through high windows, they saw a wide open space, empty except for something in the centre of the expansive concrete floor. It was a large wooden box. Sutherland drew his gun as they slowly approached, their eyes searched carefully in all directions. In the distance, Ripley could hear screeching and the faint sounds of approaching sirens echoing off the surrounding buildings.

They'll be here soon.

As they moved through the warehouse, Ripley remembered the explosion, the feeling of the pressure, the heat, the force of the blast. His heart started pounding and sweat formed on his brow, panic threatening to take hold.

"Looks like we're alone," Ripley said in a hushed voice, staring at the box which looked like an oversized coffin. He looked at Sutherland. "When the rest get here, have them tape off the entrances and stay out. We need some time alone first."

Sutherland nodded, holstered his weapon, and headed for the door. Ripley turned and slowly approached the box until he was right beside it. The smell of blood, bleach, urine, shit, and something else assailed his nostrils.

What is *that damn odour?*

He knelt down to be closer to the box. It was about seven feet long, three feet wide, and two feet deep, and was sealed with an excessive number of nails. Feeling a touch on his shoulder, Ripley turned to see Sutherland staring at the box. "We're going need some tools," Ripley said. They headed for the door to get some claw hammers, foot covers, and gloves.

Within ten minutes, they had the heavy wood cover

off the box. They were staring at a man nestled on top of a bed of hay and colourful confetti. Carefully placed next to him was a small oxygen bottle attached to a face mask covering the guy's mouth and nose, and an IV bag attached to a needle inserted in the guy's foot. Ripley stared at the medical equipment for a moment, letting it sink in, then quickly put two fingers on the man's neck. A weak pulse throbbed under his fingertips.

"He's alive! Get the fuckin' ambulance, now!" Ripley said.

Sutherland pulled out his phone and made the call. Suddenly, the victim's eyes opened and Ripley was staring into two empty, bloody sockets. He had been mutilated, his eyes scooped out. From under the oxygen mask came a wretched, weak wailing, and he started convulsing.

"Hold on, fella." A shaken Ripley did everything he could to sooth the man, placing his hand on the victim's cheek and talking to him in a calm, even tone. "Help is on the way." He didn't mess with the guy, in case he made his injuries worse, so he waited helplessly for the paramedics to arrive.

Soon there was a flurry of frantic activity as the ambulance crew did their methodical work in preparation to transport the man. Ripley and Sutherland stood back and watched, shock on their faces. As the gurney was wheeled away, Ripley noticed something else about the victim: one arm was missing. It appeared to be crudely chopped off, flesh torn and chaffed.

Once the victim was in the ambulance and on the way to St. Gabriel's, Ripley turned the scene over to the patiently waiting CSI crew. He and Sutherland had one last look over the scene before leaving for the hospital. Ripley's mind raced. Would this poor soul be able to tell them anything? What did the note at the station say? As they sped to the hospital, Ripley felt hope—and fear—that answers were close.

He gouged the sides of his knees with his fingernails, indenting his flesh and breaking slight tears in his soft skin. He immediately relaxed his hands, his mind scrolling though the consequences of broken flesh beneath his pale blue scrubs. Although blood wasn't a surprising accessory to find on the clothing of medical staff, blotches on his knees might draw some attention. And attention was what he *didn't* want. He never wanted it, never at any point, anywhere, at any time. He dropped his eyes, searching the starched fabric for signs of unwanted crimson, then dug his nails into the steering wheel of his Crown Victoria instead, resuming the pressure that stilled his mind.

People moved around him, back and forth to their vehicles, keys and coffees in hand, wearing exhaustion and apathy on their privileged faces. He would fit in well with this crowd of employees and customers, distributors and consumers of false care and temporary triage. Sure, they could stop bleeding and dull pain, but the under-lying conditions still would still remain.

Oh. to have the resources and the manpower to put this shit show to an end.

But a one man show was he, and would continue to be. For the time being, anyways.

"Time to go," he said to the single occupant of the vehicle.

He coughed, heaving a blast of air from his lungs—a calming tic—then opened the door and stepped onto the asphalt of the employee parking lot. The car door clicked shut behind him, so gently that it didn't latch. He wanted to avoid rattling himself before he smoothed out and became a presentable lost face in the crowd. He took a step, then another, casually looking around at the staff and visitors moving to and fro. They were weeping or yawning, walking hurriedly to their cars at the end of a long immersion in that building, or walking slowly to the beginning of a personal or professional shift of hell. He singled out a few people, mimicked their emotions, their actions, their nuances. A hair flick, an adjustment of the elastic waistband of the scrubs, burying faces in phones. He kept it consistent, taking care to not resemble those who were clad in street clothes or overly distraught.

Pick one side. The side that fits in. The side that can move freely without question. The side that's invisible.

He lifted his chin as he walked, widening his nostrils and pulling in air from all directions. His head turned, and he veered off course, steering away from the entrance and towards the south wall of the building. When he rounded the corner, he was pleased to find that his nose had not deceived him. A man, mid-twenties maybe, was leaned up against the brick wall, phone in hand, cigarette dangling from his lip. The man didn't hear his approach, partly because of his soft loafers, but mostly because of the grass beneath his feet. When he was suddenly upon the hidden nicotine addict, the man jumped.

"Oh, ah," the man stammered. "I just, I was only…"

He looked down at the guy's badge and flipped it over so he could read his name.

"Graham, is it?" he asked.

"Yes, and I know I shouldn't be smoking on grounds, but—"

"Let me stop you there, Graham," he said. "I'm not administration. I'm wearing fucking scrubs, you imbecile."

Graham winced, and the man waved and smirked, flashing his overly predominant teeth.

"Relax. I'm only haunting you because I want a drag."

Another wince.

"A smoke, Graham. A cigarette."

Graham heaved a sigh of relief and reached into his pocket, drawing a single Du Maurier out of his pack. He handed it over, and, for a brief moment, their hands clamped together.

"Graham, do you know why you're here?"

"Uh, I work here?"

"But here. Now."

"Because I work here, but I also smoke."

"No Graham," he said with increasing irritation. "But *here*. Now. For a reason, you think?"

Graham shifted uncomfortably.

"Graham. Are you with me Graham?"

Graham nodded. He really wasn't sure what to say.

"Well, Graham, I have to thank you."

"For what?" Graham asked.

"For what, my friend? For you!"

The man laughed from the pit of his belly, a brash and jovial laugh so sudden that it made Graham jump. The man patted Graham on the back, nearly knocking the wind out of him.

"Hey buddy," Graham said. "Knock it off."

"Oh, hey, I'm sorry. Is this better?"

The man reached out and wrapped his fingers around the back of Graham's head, and hooked his thumbs under Graham's jaw. Before Graham could react, the man twisted his head, snapping his neck like a twig. Graham crumpled silently to the ground in a heap. The man looked at him, gave his chest a little shove with the toe of his shoe, then knelt down and fished the cigarette pack from his pocket.

"Don't mind if I do," the said.

He slid the pack into the breast pocket of his own scrubs, then hauled Graham up and propped him against the brick wall. After a few manipulations, Graham looked like he could be an overworked orderly simply taking a load off after a long shift. The man yanked Graham's badge off his lanyard then walked away, turning briefly to wink in Graham's general direction.

"Have a good one. *Buddy.*"

RIPLEY WAS HAPPY HE COULDN'T HEAR THE BEEPING, THE hissing of medical machines, and the chatter and gossip behind the nurse's station. Without those noises, he could almost imagine it was simply an office building, another crime scene, or maybe a conference. But unfortunately the smell gave it away. That, and the sight of the sick and weary dragging themselves through the halls. It was business as usual around the ol' stitch 'em and ditch 'em— apathetic looking staff, angry or woeful patients, zero sense of urgency or care. Regardless of the fact that this wing was currently holding a few gunshot victims, a rape, and a near-fatal car accident, nobody seemed too excited. Same old, same old.

Ripley and Sutherland worked in a closed-off waiting area outside the ICU. The victim had been taken for surgery, and they were waiting for him to wake up so they could hopefully get something out of him. After leaving the crime scene, Ripley picked up his vehicle before they met up at the hospital to set up shop. Sutherland made phone calls, orchestrating the minions at the scene and back in the lab. Ripley didn't much like that, but phone calls were best left to the hearing. He passed the time by scrawling notes on his pad while running over the scene —well, scenes—in his mind.

Notes. Two of them with the previous victim—one dropped at the station, and one contained in the body. And the inscription AS carved into bone. The present victim was connected to one note already—also left at the station—and God knows what else inside of him. Of course it might be harder to retrieve any cutesy little messages while the mailbox was still breathing.

Did the perp mean to leave him alive? If so, that in itself is a message.

"What?" Sutherland barked across the room. "What's churning in that brain of yours?"

"Shit," Ripley said, spinning his chair around so his back was to Sutherland. He had no interest in listening to the man relieve his own stress by clucking at everyone like a rabid chicken. Ripley let the crime scenes play on the back of his eyelids—the floating red water, the confetti filled box. A hand on his shoulder. Ripley opened his eyes.

"Detective Ripley," the doctor said to his face. "I need to speak with you and detective Sutherland."

Ripley turned his seat around and placed his notebook in his lap once again. Sutherland scooted his chair up beside Ripley and the two of them looked across the table at the doctor like expectant parents fearing the worst.

"It's not good," the doctor said.

No shit, Ripley thought.

"We know," Ripley said. "We were the ones who found him."

"I'm aware of that, detective—"

"It's not detective anymore," Ripley interrupted. "Mark will be fine." Sutherland rolled his eyes.

"Okay, Mark. Obviously there's been a lot of physical trauma, but we were able to get most of that under control. No internal injuries, the arm wound had been quickly and effectively cauterized, and he wasn't in that box long enough for infection to set in. Aside from being short a wing, the main concern is his head."

"Brain injury?" Ripley said.

"I'll get to that, but no. Not exactly. His physical

injuries are obvious. The eyes were removed, rendering him blind. And his ears were tampered with."

"Tampered with?" Sutherland said.

"Yes," the doctor continued. "It was less obvious and more carefully executed than the apparent impulse job of the arm, but a procedure was performed on both ears that required a certain degree of medical precision."

"A procedure?" Mark breathed, starting to feel his head spin.

"We found blood in his ears, but scans showed no evidence of head trauma. We scoped inside the ear canal, and found that, in both ears, the malleus, incus, and stapes had been excised. There was minor damage to the cochlea, and—"

"Layman's terms, doc," Sutherland said.

"Deaf," Ripley said, beads of sweat forming above his brow.

"Yes, Mark," the doctor said. "The procedure resulted in complete deafness."

Spots floated in front of Mark's eyes. Hospitals made him moderately uncomfortable, but traumatic hearing loss was his kryptonite.

"You said something about head trauma," Sutherland said in an attempt to divert the conversation, obviously noticing Ripley's discomfort.

"Yes, well, as for any physical trauma to the brain, there appears to be none," the doctor said.

"That's good, I suppose," Sutherland said.

"This doesn't mean his head's okay," the doctor said. "He's been conscious for a bit now, and we've managed to get the appropriate physiological responses, but..."

Mark knew. Of course. What other result did they expect? Did they expect a man to endure what this guy had been through and come out psychologically unscathed on the other side?

"How bad is it?' Ripley asked.

The doctor just shook his head.

Ripley stood and held his palm out to the door.

"We'd like to see him now, doctor."

WITH HIS FEET UP ON THE COUNTER, CROSSED, TAPPING THE beat to MacIssac's latest fiddle jig, he made sure he was a quiet spectacle. That way, people would barely notice him, but if they did, they would avoid him like the plague.

"No one wants to mingle with an eccentric, now do they?" he muttered under his breath.

Nurses came and went, doctors passed by, files were grabbed and monitors viewed, but not one person really looked at him. He could feel them checking him out in their peripherals, but he was practically invisible, and wholly unapproachable. They likely thought that he was a tech or therapist of some sort, killing time between patients. He fit in quite nicely—scrubs, clipboard in hand, Graham's badge dangling from his hip. They were none the wiser, nor would they be while he was still in the building.

He fiddled with his pencil, twirling it through his fingers and composing the occasional sketch on his clipboard while waiting expectantly for the ICU to clear. It suddenly did quite the opposite, though, when the doctor and two men strode through the double doors. The door slid shut behind them, creating a barrier between him and the threesome of visitors. He started to salivate.

"Well, well, well. Look at this now," he said.

He watched the men behind the glass enter the curtained-off corner that contained his creation. Pangs of recognition warmed his blood with anticipation. He knew the doctor because he had been tending to the patent, and he knew that grimy asshole, Sutherland, but they weren't who interested him. It was *him*. *He* was here.

"Oh, how lucky can I get?" he said, smirking.

As per routine, Ripley pulled up a chair on one side of the hospital bed while Sutherland did the same on the other. Ripley motioned for Sutherland to hold back so he could take the reins. Sutherland obliged. Ripley tapped the bed, alerting the victim to their presence, then put his hand on the victim's one remaining hand.

"More," the victim muttered. "More. Finish it."

"How do we talk to him?" Sutherland whispered. "He can't hear us."

"No," Ripley said, "but he knows we're here. And he can talk. Maybe he'll come out with something on his own."

Ripley gave the victim's hand a squeeze, and the man winced and giggled, then started crying. The victim tried to pull his hand away, but restraints held his arms to the bed.

"We had to restrain him," the doctor said. "We can't sedate him any further because of the anesthetic, but he's still remarkably agitated, considering the medication in his system."

"Understandably agitated," Ripley said, keeping his eyes on the bandaged head.

"I'm not sure he understands what's happened to him," the doctor continued. "He keeps trying to tear the bandages from his eyes and the packing from his ears, as if he would be able to see and hear again."

"And you can't just remove them?" Ripley asked.

"Mark, it wouldn't feel better, you know," the doctor said, putting a hand on Ripley's shoulder. "We could take the bandages off, but the sensation of gauze would remain. As would the dark and the silence."

Ripley nodded, a lump throbbing against his Adam's apple.

"The bandages need to stay on," the doctor said. "Infection is a real risk with open wounds in such delicate areas."

The victim's head moved back and forth, his fingers twitched, and he wriggled against the restraints. He muttered something unintelligible under his breath, but the cadence and tone communicated sheer panic.

"It's okay," Mark said, placing a hand on his forehead. "You are not alone."

The man stilled, but fear washed over his face. Now he looked like a deer in headlights, one that was being watched by a road full of wolves. Ripley knew half of how that felt—how isolating and terrifying it was to be completely deprived of one of your senses. And this guy had lost two, and had probably been awake for the excruciating execution of it all. Now he didn't know what was going on—if he was okay, or what was going to happen from here on out. And he was alone. Completely and utterly alone. No familiar sight or sound to comfort him, no spouse or child or parent at his side.

Brutal.

"Sutherland," Ripley said. "Give me your badge."

"What? Why? Do us all a favour and get your own, asshole."

Ripley shot him a look. Sutherland pulled the badge

out of his pocket and tossed it across the bed. Ripley picked it up, flipped open the cover, and placed it in the victim's hand. He moved the victim's fingers over the shield several times until the man started doing it on his own.

"Police," the man said.

Ripley patted his hand in acknowledgement. Sutherland raised an eyebrow and nodded.

"Clever cock," Sutherland said.

"Gone," the victim said.

Ripley stared at the victim for a moment, then tapped his hand to prompt him on.

"Hear no evil, see no evil... BOOM! No evil!" The victim's voice becoming snide and hateful. "No amount of duct tape will patch this one up, no!"

Ripley looked at Sutherland, and Sutherland looked at the doctor.

"Like I said," sighed the doctor, "there isn't any physical brain damage. Psychologically, however, he's completely broken."

"I don't want it. I don't want you, or them, or him," the victim said. "I want it, okay? I want it! I want to ascend the leg of humanity, crawl right back into that pussy and plant myself in the womb of creation, rebirth myself with a clean slate, like he said!"

The victim's laughs rang out, peppered with choking sobs. The doctor summoned a nurse to grab a cold cloth and Ripley attempted to soothe him. His breathing slowed, and he tilted his head towards Ripley.

"I will still see with my heart," the victim sputtered.

He sobbed and buried his head into Ripley's chest.

HE SAT ON AN EMPTY BED IN THE CURTAINED CUBICLE adjacent to the one that his creation occupied—the one that contained the three amigos who were sticking their noses where noses didn't belong.

"I don't want it. I don't want you, or them—"

He listened as his creation droned on, wagging that ever-loving fucking tongue of his. How could he say those things, and with such a tone?

Heathen.

He didn't understand the utilitarian consequences of their work together.

Stupid bastard.

Even so, he is but a mere sheep, and a powerful messenger. Just not with his damn mouth, evidently.

He slipped away, out the double doors and down the hallway. After grabbing a couple items from a nearby nursing cart, he walked the ward until he arrived at the furthest room, then grabbed the chart off the door and gave it a quick review before entering.

"Well hello, Mrs. Irving! I'm doctor Graham..."

~

ALARMS WENT OFF, AND SUTHERLAND AND THE DOCTOR rushed to the door. Ripley lifted his head away from the victim and looked at Sutherland.

"Alarm," Sutherland said.

Ripley looked at the doctor.

"It's a code," the doctor said. "I'm going to have to ask you guys to leave the room. This is a restricted area, and you can't be here without medical staff present."

"Of course," Ripley said, patting the shuddering victim on the arm. "I think we're done here anyways."

The three passed through the double doors, and the doctor motioned to the cordoned off waiting room.

"Are you guys going to head back there?"

"Yeah," Sutherland said. "We need to have a little powwow before we clear out. Take your time."

The doctor joined the flow of medical staff heading down the hallway to the code in question. Sutherland walked into their makeshift work area as Ripley stood staring through the doors of the ICU.

Fuck.

He looked in at the curtained cubicle, trying very hard not to imagine what it was like for that poor man.

A sudden impact jolted him back to the present when

a man pushing a cart through the double doors ran right into him.

"Sorry," the man said. "So sorry."

The man reached out and grasped Ripley's shoulder, giving it a firm squeeze as he passed by.

Ripley nodded, then dipped his head and went to join Sutherland.

HE PULLED THE SURGICAL MASK OVER THE LOWER HALF OF his face and gripped the cart with both hands. As he got closer, his whole body started to tingle with excitement. Close, closer still, the squeaky wheels of the cart going unnoticed by his new friend. He steered the cart around the pseudo-detective, but made sure to bump him.

"Sorry. So sorry," he said to his new friend, daring to reach out and grab his shoulder. He squeezed, and felt the life within the other man, the flesh beneath his clothes, the connection between him and this man—his kindred spirit. The man barely looked up to see who had collided with him.

Lost in thought, I suppose.

He wheeled the cart into the ICU, into the cubicle, and pulled the curtain shut behind him. His creation stilled very suddenly as the cart came to a rest beside his bed. His mouth tightened and his face crumpled into a sob.

"You," the creation hissed. "I smell you."

Of course you do. You are evolving, and your nose is your eyes, now. Good work, lad. Good work.

"Okay, sir," he said to his creation. "I know you can't hear me, but I still need to walk you through the procedure. Ethics, you know."

The man reached over and disabled the alarms and monitors, then picked up a scalpel from the cart.

"So the guy has the mental capacity of a butternut squash," Sutherland said.

Ripley gave him a hard look, and Sutherland shrugged his shoulders.

"Well? I don't blame him, of course. I'd wish myself dead, if it were me."

"Be that as it may," Ripley said, "he probably doesn't have the mental fortitude left to even contemplate suicide."

"It's tragic," Sutherland said, sitting down beside Ripley and putting a hand on his knee, "and this must be tough on you. How are you holding up?"

Ripley couldn't stifle a laugh.

"What is this?" Ripley asked. "You? Giving a shit?"

Sutherland pushed Ripley's knee away and gave his shoulder a gentle punch. "You know, I do care about you, despite all the emotional abuse you put me through."

"Me?" Ripley scoffed.

Sutherland was an asshole, but Ripley was no saint himself. There were moments, fleeting glimpses of camaraderie that kept him coming back to his friend for more. Despite the turmoil of the past, Sutherland had always been there. He had been a consistent friend through the bad and the worse, and for that, Ripley was extremely grateful. Even if he wanted to sock the guy in the junk every now and then.

The men gathered their things and made their way to the elevators. The doctor had been gone for almost an hour, and they didn't need anything more at the moment, anyhow. Ripley left a note for him at the triage desk to let him know to contact the station with any developments, but both he and Sutherland knew the hospital housed nothing more than dead ends. They would head back to the station and wait for the evidence to come back on the crate and the warehouse.

"You parked outside?" Sutherland asked.

"Yeah. I like the air, especially after being stuck in here. Don't you?"

"Naw, I like the parkade. My paranoia draws me towards surveillance cameras."

Ripley nodded and gave Sutherland a quick salute

before exiting the elevator on the main floor. As Ripley walked out the front door towards his car, he felt a slight pressure on his chest. The world around him began to constrict, and his breathing became shallow. He felt the blood pounding in his ears and pulsating behind his eyes. Black spots started making an appearance on the very edge of his peripheral. Ripley hated it when this happened, when the silence threatened to swallow him whole. The world was so big and so busy, but so silent. It was claustrophobic. He saw people everywhere around him—walking and talking, eating, punching fat fingers on cell phones—but Ripley felt like he was gliding across the bottom of the ocean. He needed to get somewhere safe, somewhere secure. Somewhere that was *supposed* to be quiet. Panic threatened to win the race, so Ripley upped the pace a tad, making it to his car at a near-run. He slid behind the wheel, locked himself in, and leaned his seat back until he was almost fully reclined.

"Calm down," he commanded himself.

He took deep breaths in through his nose, then opened his mouth to release the air and tension. A few more centering breaths and his heart begin to slow. He laid there for a good ten minutes, allowing his eyelids to rest over his eyes and cherishing the senses he had left. When he finally felt he was steady enough to drive safely back to the station—or home for a rest if he had any sense—he raised his seat back up and reached into his pocket for his keys. As his hands trailed to the ignition, his eyes drifted to his passenger seat.

A gift box, bright yellow and sealed with a green bow, sat quietly beside him, a terrifying passenger. Ripley looked out his windows, searching for anyone who looked suspicious, but saw only people wearing scrubs and morose people with their heads tucked into their chests. Typical hospital clientele. He looked back at the box.

He knew he shouldn't touch it. He knew he should immediately call Sutherland, get some back up—maybe even the bomb squad—and get back behind the lines while someone else opened the fucking thing. Ripley knew that. But his fingers reached out anyways, teasing the ribbon between his thumb and finger until it loosened enough for him to slide it off the box. He bit his lower lip and lifted the lid.

The box was arranged like a nest. Mark leaned in closer, examining the ivory tissue paper that was drenched in a deep, wet crimson. He pulled the paper aside to get a good look at the contents of the box.

Fresh. So fresh it was still glistening. A large, freshly severed tongue. And on the broad surface of the meat, a message was carved.

Silence.

CHAPTER 7

He sat stock still, barely containing a gleeful giggle. Crouched deep in the shadows behind the wheel of his Crown Victoria, he studied the obviously distressed Ripley who had just got into his fancy classic Ford.

Try to figure that one out, pretend cop!

He'd done a little digging and found out the guy's name was Mark Ripley, and that he was stone cold deaf from an accident on the force. He used to be a cop, but had quit after said accident.

It's interesting that they trust him to take the lead on this case.

Ripley obviously had some cred with the force. He even seemed to be the boss over that asshole Sutherland who was, surprisingly, still a cop. *I wonder what that's all about?*

Keeping his eyes on Ripley in his car, his mind drifted joyfully back to the events in the hospital.

Tied off loose ends! Yes I did! He smiled big and gave himself a mental pat on the back.

Try and get something out of him now.

The job had been simple: create a distraction to clear the room and get 'er done. He was proud of his ability to knock the creation out with drugs, cut out the tongue, and still keep him alive. And he was just as excited—if not more so—about his close encounter with Ripley in the hall. He loved the feeling of his hand on Ripley's shoulder.

I'm gonna be paying attention to you, dude. Just you wait and see.

The hardest part was carving a clear word in that tongue. He'd done it in his car with the scalpel he'd used to excise the organ. It was a slow job, but clearly readable when he was finished. The box for presentation he'd had in his trunk, fully prepared for an event like this. He smiled again.

I am one brilliant son of a bitch! He grinned at his own genius. *Deaf, dumb and blind! The creation is nearly perfect in this god-awful world!*

His eyed bored into Ripley's car, studying the man's every movement. Getting into the car to leave his prize was easy. *Thank God for the internet.* He'd learned the skills to quickly break into a vehicle long ago, and an old car like a Fairlane? Piece of cake.

Suddenly, he saw commotion and thrashing around in Ripley's car. The prize was found! Still as a mouse and barely breathing, he watched in fascination, his mouth open, drooling in anticipation of what would happen next.

RIPLEY STARED IN ABJECT HORROR, AND HIS STOMACH rolled violently. Throwing the door wide open, he leaned over and threw his guts up onto the black asphalt below. Staggering clumsily out of the car, he kept heaving until all that remained was foul-tasting bile in his mouth and an acrid stinging in his throat. Finally, his heart slowed and his stomach began to settle. Grabbing his cell, he texted Sutherland.

Get back here now. Parking lot.

Sutherland must have just rolled out of the parkade. Within a few minutes he was beside Ripley, staring at the package. "You shouldn't have touched that, dumbass," he said gently, knowing Ripley was in a bad state.

"Call in the crime scene guys and I'll get back to that hospital room," Ripley said. "You come up after they get here."

Sutherland complied. Ripley hurried back to the hospital, his head pounding and his gut turning over in protest. When he arrived back at the victim's room, he found mass confusion. Everyone was racing around trying to keep the guy from bleeding out.

It his *tongue, all right. How in the Hell did this happen right under our noses?*

Ripley cautioned the staff to touch as little as possible in the room, then escaped to the hall to wait.

IT ALL FINALLY SETTLED. THE VICTIM WAS STABLE AND quiet, fully sedated. Ripley sat in the hall, holding his pounding head, when Sutherland arrived out of breath. "CSI guys are here. They're pissed that you opened the box."

Ripley nodded in defeat. "The perp was right here in front of us." He shook his head, trying to clear the creeping fog that had entered. "He's got us beat at every turn."

Sutherland studied Ripley's face. Ripley was as white as a ghost, which made his scar stand out like a flashing neon sign. In a rare gesture of compassion, Sutherland sat beside him, placing a meaty hand on Ripley's shoulder. "We'll get him, buddy. All these perps eventually make a mistake."

They sat together, silently thinking about the crazy events of the day, when a cop came running from the elevator. "Another body, guys. Outside the hospital. Our men are cordoning off the area so you guys can check it out." He looked at Ripley. "The CSI team will move there when they're finished with your car."

Ripley glanced at Sutherland. "Let's get down there," Forgetting about feelings of failure, they hurried down to the main floor and around the corner of the hospital, led by the officer who had retrieved them.

The corpse was a young man in hospital scrubs with a burned out cigarette beside his open palm. It was obvious from the angle of the man's head that someone had broken his neck. Ripley searched for an ID tag, but found nothing.

"That's how our perp got access," Ripley said. "He took this guy's tag." They looked the scene over, careful not to disturb anything, then left it for the rest of the crew to examine.

Heading back upstairs, they found the CSI team carefully examining the victim's room, which was now closed off with yellow police tape. The doctor was there, shaking his head, talking to a few nurses. He made eye contact with Ripley, shaking his head.

Didn't make it.

Sitting back on the bench they had just left minutes earlier, Ripley's ploughed ahead. "We need to see all the security videos for today. Our guy's got to be there some-where." He got up, re-energized. "Sutherland, you head back to the office and check out what the CSI guys have found so far. I'm going to spend time here checking out all the security videos for today."

"Okay, buddy. Good luck." Sutherland turned and headed for the elevators.

Ripley was quickly directed to the security office and, after some instruction from the security personnel, was left alone to study the recordings.

"He's got to be here somewhere,"

Ripley muttered to himself. He soon found the video showing sporadic surveillance of the floor. He settled in, carefully examining everyone moving in and out of the scene.

SUTHERLAND ARRIVED BACK NEXT TO RIPLEY'S CAR. THE CSI guys had finished up and released the scene. Except for the vomit next to the car, everything seemed back to normal. He jumped in his black and white and made his way back to headquarters.

Before long, Sutherland found himself in the pres-ence of Doctor Jackie Fields. He knew Fields and Ripley could have a thing going on, but that didn't stop him from fantasizing. In his mind's eye, he pictured all kinds of scenes starring him and Fields as the main characters.

Ah well, maybe later.

He focused on the tongue, which was displayed on a stainless steel tray in Field's hand.

"The tongue was surgically removed by a very sharp instrument," Field's said. "Likely a scalpel. And the word carved into it had to be done with a scalpel as well, looks to be the same grade. The guy would have needed time and a solid background to do it properly."

Sutherland stared at the word, 'SILENCE', carved into the tongue. The vic's eyes, his hearing, and his tongue were all gone. It was like the perp wanted to remove all of his senses...

Thanking Fields, Sutherland headed back to his office to think. His discussions with the CSI team had produced nothing of value yet, so they were almost back to square one. All they really had was the strange blood type, the carved AS, and the surveillance videos. Since Ripley was taking care of the videos, Sutherland decided to concentrate on narrowing the field further on the blood type. He set to work with a vengeance, working on his own, personal task.

RIPLEY'S BRAIN WAS NUMB. STARING AT THE VIDEOS, HIS

eyes crossed from stress and fatigue. Because of privacy laws, there were no cameras in the patient rooms. This left Ripley sifting through a plethora of video to determine which people *might* have gone towards the victim's room. Ripley's stomach had settled, and he realized he hadn't eaten for what felt like years. Sudden, ravenous hunger surged through his body, so he headed for the cafeteria, making sure the security office was guarded by a remaining officer.

Wolfing down a burger and fries, Ripley looked up as one of the guys from security came over, carrying his own tray of carbs and fat.

"Mind if I sit?" the young guy asked. Ripley pointed at the empty chair across from him, and soon the guy was chomping and talking at the same time. "You know," he said, "I may be able to help you speed up your search of the videos."

"How's that?" Ripley asked.

"I can narrow time frames very quickly. If you give me probable times and locations, I can scope out the important stuff for you, ya know, weirdos or outsiders coming and going. I know the regulars, and—"

"Eat up. Your coming back with me. I need a little efficiency."

After finishing their lunch, they walked together back to the security room and sat down as Ripley studied his notes. "All right. The perp must have entered the victim's room somewhere around 3:30 PM, just after that alarm went off. Let's look at that area's recording for around that time."

"No problem." Soon the video was playing the approximate time. Ripley studied each person meandering the halls.

"Sorry we can't see right into the ICU. HEPA prevents us from putting cameras anywhere but at nurses stations and hall exits—"

"Wait! Back it up a bit and slow it down if you can.

"You got it," the security guy responded. He backed it up and let it run at a very slow speed.

"Stop," Ripley ordered. They were staring at the back of a young man with short, dark hair. He was wearing hospital scrubs and walking purposefully towards the ICU, pushing a tray.

Gooseflesh swelled on Ripley's skin as a vision played in the back of his mind: a man in a mask, bumping him, touching his arm, scurrying by him with a cart...

"Back it up slowly. I need to see his face," Ripley said through gritted teeth.

"You got it man." He backed up the video until the person of interest was out of the scene. Then he let it go forward at a snail's pace. No face. The guy kept his face turned away from the camera.

Clever.

"We'll see if his face shows when he leaves." Ripley

anxiously stared at the video as the doors to the ICU opened and closed. No one else entered.

After a while, the guy came back out, wearing a surgical mask and carrying something in a plastic bag. *The tongue.* Ripley swallowed, bile rising from his stomach. Soon the guy was gone towards the elevators.

"Back it up again. I need the best view with his face toward the camera." Soon he was looking at a still shot. He studied it carefully. *Something familiar.* He looked at the security guy. "Can you capture that image and print it out for me?"

"No problemo," the guy responded, and soon Ripley had a glossy black-and-white photo in his hand. He placed it under a desk lamp and studied the face carefully. There was something very familiar about it, even with the mask.

Now having a bit of an idea what he looked like, Ripley asked the security guy to go back over other videos to find someone with similar hair, build, and features that they could see. Maybe they could find the guy without his mask.

After exhaustive searching, they were looking at an earlier video of the nurse's station. They focused on a man sitting with his feet up on the desk, toes tapping along to some merry tune. He was wearing the same scrubs as the man who went in the room, and his hair was the same.

Ripley froze.

No. It can't be.

He just about passed out on the spot. Getting a grip on himself, he dismissed the security guy and sat there, staring in dread at the image on the monitor. The guy's hair was a bit different, the image was grainy, but the resemblance was uncanny.

What in the Hell is going on?

Ripley had the security guard print out this photo as well, and slowly headed to the elevators, his shaky legs barely supporting the weight of his body. His head reeled and acid burned up his trachea, a resurgence of digestive stress that he thought he had left behind at his car hours earlier.

No. It can't be. Tommy, tell me it isn't you.

The bar hummed with a tangle of white noise; an entwined chorus of clinking glasses, mumbled conversation, and raucous tunes were belted out by a mullet-sporting cover band. But all Ripley could do was feel the chaos, a cacophony of vibrations, sights, and smells assaulting his senses. People moved around in swarms, balancing cellphones and pints, oozing charm and swagger. Ripley pushed through the crowd, every touch shooting pangs of irritation straight through to his core. The flashing lights and noxious odors of smoke and whiskey and weed were almost too much for him to handle. However, his lack of hearing had one upside, and this place was a classic example. He wasn't overwhelmed by the noise that undoubtedly emanated from the speakers and undesirable crowd. That, and he didn't have to strain to hear conversational partners.

"Is he here?" Ripley shouted across the booze-tacky bar at the brooding barkeep.

"Somewhere," Randall replied, continuing to pour pints as he maintained eye contact with Ripley.

"Well, where?" Ripley asked, impatience stewing in his tone.

"In the bar," Randall answered. Even without being able to hear his tone, Ripley knew it was sour. Ripley ran his hands through his hair and scoured the bar. So many people, so many lights, so much bullshit. A touch on his shoulder drew his attention back to the barkeep.

"Hey, can I get you a drink while you wait?" Randall said. "It's on the house."

Ripley nodded, and the lumbering man mixed up a whiskey sour. Ripley examining the knots on the wood of the bar. Finally, Randall slid the drink close to Ripley's face, and Ripley looked up once again. Randall's face was full of pity. Ripley hated that.

"Hey man," Randall said. "He flits through periodically like a hummingbird on meth. Shouldn't be long until he passes by here again. If any of us see him, we'll tell him you're here."

"Thanks," Ripley said, raising his glass to cheers Randall. Randall lifted his own shot of top shelf whiskey and pounded it back in one gulp before moving on to the next customer.

Ripley watched. He watched people moving about, chatting lustfully with strangers, stabbing sharp words at enemies, shooting the shit with buddies. He thought of his life, or lack thereof, and all the relationships he had abandoned after the accident. He spent most nights distracting himself from crippling loneliness with first player shooters or getting lost in fantasy realms, but now this maniac had him occupied. Whether that was a good thing remained to be seen, but at least he was out mingling in the land of the living.

After leaving the hospital, he had gone and paced around the cop shop for a while, trying to piece together what his eyes were trying to tell him. The more time that passed, the less be believed it had been his son on that video. His son, sitting in that chair, pushing that steel cart...

Sutherland had been his usual self, lazing about, picking at minor investigations that would ultimately unearth more questions than answers. When Ripley had finally left the station shortly before dinner, Sutherland was playing a rousing game of hurry up and wait, skulking around the lab to see the results of the impending blood work and fingerprint analysis from samples retrieved at the hospital. That, and trying to get as much face time as possible with Jackie Fields.

Asshole, Ripley thought. *The one woman in my life. My only chance at another relationship.*

Ripley scowled. Sutherland was a social butterfly, flitting about the world effortlessly, inundated with a plethora of opportunity, and all he did was hone in on the one woman, the *only* woman, that Ripley fancied. Ripley quickly shrugged off his bitterness. As much as he adored Jackie, he knew he didn't have a chance with her. He was so caught up in his own little world, and was subsequently so moody and removed that he doubted she would ever show a glimmer of interest in him. Besides, he'd never have the balls to try.

Ripley finished off his whiskey. Then another. And another. Time crawled by like a slug moving the hand of a clock, leaving a fog of drunken slime behind it. The lights and the colors wobbled the more Ripley drowned his stress, and soon he was feeling that familiar numbness he always hoped would save him from his world of hurt. But instead of dulling his anxieties, it amplified them; he became acutely aware of his shortcomings, the suffocating world around him, and the life that had slipped from between his fingers. Ripley had traveled this path before, letting the drink take on the role of therapist, and the bill was a hefty dose of deeper depression and anxiety. *Whatever*, he thought. *Damned if I do, and damned if I don't.*

⁓

A WHISKEY SOUR, TOP SHELF NO LESS. DICK'S GOT CASH, THAT'S for sure. How does it taste on those sour lips? How does the sound of your drowned sorrows ring in your ears? Do you feel like you're drowning, or simply rising up for air? You don't know how grateful you should be to have your blessing.

He sat across the room, hidden by drunken two-steppers and an archaic jukebox standing simply for looks rather than function. He had followed Ripley, first to the station and then to this place, a beverage trough for the ill-repute. He was a tad disappointed in Ripley's choice of establishment. He had pegged him for more of a middle-class drunk, not one of these pub crawlers that liked to wallow in the spit and filth and sweat of minimum wage lemmings gyrating and sloshing about the floor like farm animals. No, there was something else, some other reason Ripley chose this place to tip his glass.

He looked around, scanning the scum and the horny masses, trying to seek the source of Ripley's interest. Ripley was no help. He didn't seem to be focused on anything besides his glass and the burly bartender.

Is he meeting someone? Yes. That has to be it.

He directed his attention to the door, leaving Ripley and his drink unmonitored at the bar. People came and people went, but no one of any particular worth. He knew he was risking everything by coming here—by trailing this newfound mate. But he couldn't help himself. Mark Ripley was in his blood now, and he was truly addicted.

A patron, a staggering bloke adorned in a stained tank top and ripped jeans, stumbled into him and knocked him to the floor. He looked up at the mess of a man, then down at the puddle in which he lay. Alcohol, a stray french fry or two, spit, some other bodily fluids...

"Hey man," the drunken orangoutang sputtered, offering his hand as assistance. "My bad."

He winced, noting the filth caked under the cockroach's yellowed nails, and stood under his own power. He looked around at the seat of his neatly tailored trousers, wincing at the moisture that soiled the fine-grain wool. He felt heat rise in his brain and his eye began to twitch. His ears hummed as rage bubbled beneath his neatly groomed exterior. The drunken idiot wavered on his feet and ran his hands through his greasy ponytail.

"Oh gawd. You're a mess now in those purdy clothes. Sorry pal."

He cringed, digging his fingernails into his palms, and looked the idiot straight in the eye. The man winced when, even in his drunken stupor, he saw the rage burning deep within the other man's soul.

"Hey look," the drunk said. "'Twas an accident. Chill the fuck out. Maybe if you had been payin' attention, not battin' those queer lashes at all the boys in the bar, maybe your pants woulda stayed dry."

The drunk's friends erupted into raucous laughter.

"I'm sorry sir," he said, his senses now completely dulled. "You are truly mistaken. I have about as much interest in anyone here as I would a leper colony. Good day to you."

And with that, he clenched his fist and threw a right hook that landed square against the bridge of the drunk's nose. Blood spouted like Old Faithful, and he dropped to the floor, clutching his face and gagging on the blood pouring down his throat. A split second later, the drunk's buddies were in a pile on the floor, swinging and wrestling with the two men, and the bouncers had joined in on the fun.

THE PATRONS SURROUNDING RIPLEY TURNED THEIR HEADS, fascinated by a brawl that had broken out on the far side of the bar. Ripley gave it a quick glance, then simply let it blend in with the rest of the visual noise around him.

Animals.

He was borderline drunk, but at least he knew to keep his words in his mouth and his fists in his pockets. He had the benefit, though, of not being able to hear the bullshit that was spewed his way, so his level of irritation remained relatively low at most times.

After a few minutes, the ruckus quieted, the offending parties having been effectively removed from the premises. Ripley signaled Randall for another round, but the large man shook his head, and pointed beyond Ripley's shoulder. Ripley turned, and was greeted by a set of pale blue eyes and a gleaming white smile.

"Dad," Tommy said, extending his hand for a shake.

Ripley looked down. Tommy's hand was coated in fresh blood, his knuckles scuffed and swollen. Tommy noticed too, and quickly withdrew his handshake.

"Damn dicks," Tommy said. "C'mon back to my apartment while I get changed and washed up. Maybe we can have a bite to eat together?"

"That'd be nice," Ripley said.

RIPLEY SAT ON A LARGE LEATHER SOFA PERUSING MAGAZINES while his son had a shower and changed his clothes. Ripley was on edge, but slowly simmered as he looked his son over from head to toe. Tall, handsome, close cropped hair and designer clothes. He was a good kid, and an even better man.

"Geez, dad," Tommy said, rubbing his head. "You look like you've seen a ghost. Everything okay?"

No, son. Not really.

"Yeah, Tommy," Ripley said. "Sorry, it's just been a long day. At least I don't get roughed up at my job. Not any more, at least."

Tommy offered an uncomfortable smirk, and both men looked down at their feet. It was difficult for Ripley to talk to Tommy about the explosion and what had become of his life. The divorce had an impact on Tommy, he was sure, but not as much as watching his father's downward spiral into depression and isolation. Tommy had been loving, tolerant, and supportive, all while trying to grow into a man. Ripley's eyes dampened with tears as he thought of how he had let his son down. Tommy sat beside him on the sofa and put an arm around his shoulders.

"It's okay, Dad," Tommy said. "I'm fine, and so are you. Hell, I own my own bar. I'm bringing in cash hand over fist. And you're working. You're on the go every day, living, breathing, existing. Dad, we could have lost you."

"I guess you kind of did, in a way," Ripley said, tears threatening to flow. "I'm sorry I've been so detached."

Tommy hugged him. "Dad, of course you are. Trauma does that to a person. You will recover, in time, but you have to let people in."

Ripley nodded and patted his son on the knee. No more words would come without the floodgates opening.

"Besides, I'm not sure how you haven't gone bat-shit

insane, seeing the stuff that you see," Tommy said as he stood and made his way over to the minibar to pour a pair of drinks. "What have you got on the burner, now?"

Right, Ripley thought to himself. *I thought I had you, son. But now, seeing you in person...*

"What have you been up to, Tommy?" Ripley asked. He wasn't sure how Tommy would take his avoidance, but likely he would figure that Ripley couldn't talk about an ongoing case. There had been a lot of that throughout his life.

"Not too much. This place has me run ragged, most times. Sixteen-hour days, seven days a week. We just lost our floor manager, so I've been covering. And we're short a few bouncers—lost them when they crawled back to colleges across the country—so I'm throwing my muscle around out there as well," Tommy said, giving another weak smirk and flashing his battered knuckles at Ripley.

"Where were you this morning?" Ripley asked, trying to sound as nonchalant as possible.

Judging by the look on Tommy's face, Ripley had come across as the complete opposite. The two stared each other down for an uncomfortable moment, then Tommy broke the silence with a blast of defense.

"Dad, you know I'm not wrapped up in that anymore."

"I know son, I'm not suggesting—"

"Of course you are!" Tommy sighed and rubbed his

temples. "That'll plague me for the rest of my life. One slip up, my moment of weakness as our world fell apart. I used, I sold, I made enough green to finance this bar, but now it's all over. I'm clean, and that business is in the past."

"Tommy, this has nothing to do with the drugs."

"Well what then?"

"I'm just curious what you've been up to."

"Specifically this morning?"

Ripley sighed.

"I'm working a case right now," Ripley admitted. "It's messed up. *Really* messed up. I'm just worried. I... I thought I saw you on surveillance. I'm just concerned, and I don't want you around all of that mess."

Tommy paused, searching his father's face, then his expression softened.

"That job's really fucking with your head, Dad."

Ripley nodded and smiled at Tommy, trying to lighten the heaviness that now hung in the space between them.

"I was here this morning," Tommy said, "working the books with Randall."

Ripley raised an eyebrow.

"Randall is that brute tending bar out there. The one with the sloped brow and biceps bigger than tree trunks."

"Ah. Randall. Well I guess I needn't worry about you if that's the company you're keeping."

Tommy laughed and directed his attention back to the empty glasses begging to be filled.

"Yeah, I slept here on the couch last night—late night slinging shots—and he met me here half-past eight to review our ledgers. We try to do that every couple weeks or so. A place like this is under the tax man's microscope, what with the tips and off-the-books employees and all."

"Of course, of course," Ripley said. He felt like a Buick had been lifted from his shoulders, and he accepted the beverage his son thrust in his direction. With a raise of their glasses, they clinked and cheered.

"To us, and to renewed life," Tommy said.

"Indeed," Ripley replied, lifting his glass and savoring the strong liquor on his lips.

TOMMY WATCHED HIS DAD SLEEPING HEAVILY ON THE SOFA, the brown leather stuck to the side of his sunken face. He looked terrible. Tommy felt a certain measure of guilt— guilt for what he didn't do, guilt for what he couldn't. At one time he had thought that his dad might bounce back from what happened: from the accident, the dissolution of his marriage, from himself. But now, as time passed, Tommy wasn't so sure anymore. The shell of a man before him had only burrowed deeper into a hole, so deep that Tommy thought he would soon not be able to reach in and pull him out.

One drink had turned into a bottle, then two. Tommy could hold his liquor—hell, he ran a bar—but his dad couldn't keep up.

Best thing, probably. Better passed out on the couch than driving home half in the bag.

Although still upright, Tommy felt a touch woozy himself. After wavering about the toilet and relieving himself, he stood at the sink to wash his hands and stared at his reflection in the mirror. Although younger and more muscular, he didn't look much better than his father. His skin was pale and grey, his eyes buried in deep, dark sockets. Tommy shuddered and opened the mirror so he didn't have to look at himself.

There. There it was, calling to him, beckoning him. Tommy had no reason to resist. It had gotten him where he was today, and there were much worse places to be. By the looks of his father, he would need to support him financially in the near future, and this allowed Tommy the means with which to do that very thing. He reached for the vial, feeling it's cold glass in his hands, and set it on the counter. He reached into the drawer for a syringe and hesitated.

"First thing's first," he mumbled under his breath.

He set the vial down on the counter, flipped open his cell phone, and pressed the first speed dial.

"Randall. I need to talk to you about this morning. About the books *I did with you*," Tommy said.

RIPLEY WOKE TO SCATHING SUNLIGHT GLOWING THROUGH his eyelids, his head a swimming mess of pain and fog. He sat up abruptly, his face stuck to a tacky pile of drool puddled on the leather sofa beneath him. It took him a full few minutes to gain his bearings and realize where he was.

"Tommy," he whispered under his breath.

Ripley stood and looked himself over, surveying the damage, and strolled through the apartment to see if his son was around.

Nope. Already gone for the day.

Ripley poured a glass of water from the fridge and sat at the table. He looked around the apartment, admiring how clean and orderly it was. Tommy was clean and organized, and a hell of a businessman to boot. A sense of pride filled his chest, but also guilt.

How could I have even considered that Tommy could have done those horrible things?

Ripley deduced that his mind was, in fact, deteriorating to a pickled state of mush—from stress, from booze, from the blast. He saw Tommy in that video because his twisted mind wanted him to see Tommy.

"You're such a judgmental asshole, Ripley. Get yourself together."

How much longer could he competently work cases? At what point would he need to say fuck it all and check himself into a facility for some help?

Not yet. I can work through this, smarten myself up.

Ripley startled as his leg vibrated, and he reached into his pants and retrieved his cellphone. It was a text message from Sutherland.

Get here. To the station. Now.

Ripley's stomach did a flip. He swished his mouth out with water and hit the road.

SUTHERLAND STOOD, SWEAT ON HIS BROW, A PIECE OF paper crumpled in his clenched fist. The lab tech braced himself for a yell, or possibly even a physical blow. Sutherland looked like he was on the verge of eruption.

"You sure about this?" Sutherland said through clenched teeth. "Run it again!"

"I did," the meek lab mouse squeaked. "Three times, actually. I knew you'd question the results—"

"Of course I question the results, you incompetent simpleton!"

Sutherland took a deep breath and closed his eyes. *It's*

not this idiot's fault, he told himself. *He's only running the program and interpreting the numbers.*

Sutherland left the lab, making a straight and hurried line for Ripley's nest in the conference room. Once inside, he shut the door and plunked himself down at the table. He smoothed out the crumpled paper in his fist and read it again. And again.

"Goddamnit, Mark. You going to be able to handle this, ol' friend?"

CHAPTER 9

The door to the conference room crashed open. "What's the big emergency, Sutherland?" Ripley demanded, agitation written all over his face.

Sutherland knit his bushy eyebrows, scowled, and pointed to the empty chair across the table. His face was white and his eyes bloodshot.

He looks sickly. Stressed. This is really getting to him.

"You're gonna need to sit down for this," Sutherland said, smoothing out the wrinkled paper, looking irritated. "We got the DNA analysis from the blood on the notes. Not only is it a rare blood type—AB negative—but there's a familial match."

"A familial match?" Ripley sat staring, puzzled by the wrinkled paper on the table. He grabbed it, flipping it around and reading through the detailed information. Then he read it again, his jaw dropping to his lap. "This can't be!" He shot a penetrating look into Sutherland's eyes. "There's got to be some kind of colossal mistake. Have them run it again."

"They checked it three times," Sutherland sneered.

Sutherland looked uncomfortable. Ripley's face darkened. The results were abundantly clear; the blood analysis showed a familial match to his own family. That meant the blood used in the notes was from himself, Sarah, or Tommy. There could be no other explanation.

"Well?" Sutherland growled. "I know the perp's not you or Sarah. You're not AB negative, and she's, well, a *she*. That leaves Tommy. You *know* that video from the hospital showed a guy that looked damn close to Tommy."

Ripley squirmed in his chair, feeling nauseous. "That wasn't Tommy." His voice sounded like he was pleading. "Tommy has an alibi for the time that video was taken. He was working on the books for the bar."

"How do you know? Just because he said so?"

Ripley's temper flared. "No, his business partner was there with him!"

Sutherland squinted his eyes and snarled. "Have you checked the alibi out? Is there any doubt?"

Ripley's face fell. "No, I haven't. I just believed what Tommy told me." The scar across his face reddened, pulsing like a beacon. "I can't believe Tommy's involved. He's been clean for a long time, and he runs a profitable business. He's got his act together, and this kind of crazy behaviour is just not him. I believe him." Ripley braced himself. He knew what Sutherland was about to say.

"You never checked his god-damned alibi? What kind of asshole pseudo-cop have you become? You used to be meticulous with detailed crap like that, and you gave me grief about it so many times about sloppy work when you were on the force."

"I know," Ripley said, feeling properly chastised. "Look Dale, I've been going through a rough patch lately. No excuse. I'll check out the alibi right now."

"No you won't," Sutherland said, shaking his head. "In fact you should be pulled off the case. You're too close. *I'll* check the alibi. If it's rock solid, then we start looking elsewhere. If not, you and I need to talk to Captain Sloan about your involvement in all of this." He glared at Ripley as he grabbed his jacket and headed for the door. "You stay here until this is cleared up one way or another!" He stomped out, slamming the door behind him.

Ripley hung his pounding head in shame. He felt dizzy, like he was going to pass out.

No more damn booze.

Uncertainty plagued him. Tommy had gone through a bad stretch with drug addiction and drug dealing as a teenager and young adult. He'd even ended up in jail for a stint. But when he got out, he seemed to have changed his ways, and had been doing great ever since...

Or has he?

The blood on the notes, AB negative. If that was from Tommy, then everything changed. A sample of his blood was needed immediately. That would put all this bullshit to rest. Depending on what Sutherland found out about the alibi, seeking further blood tests would be next. But how was he going to approach Tommy and Sarah without everything blowing up in his face?

Plotting in his mind how things would proceed, his mind descended into deep depression. He felt like a total failure. Stewing in his emotional distress, Ripley was startled when the door opened and Dr. Jackie Fields peeked in. "Hi Mark, can we talk for a minute?" Jackie smiled softly.

Jumping unsteadily to his feet, Ripley replied, "Of course. Come in and have a seat."

Sitting quietly across from Ripley, Jackie reached across and put her hand gently over his. Her beautiful, emerald green eyes showed deep concern and empathy. "Mark, I know about the familial match in the DNA. This must be a real shock to you."

Ripley felt himself starting to break down. A tear edged out of the corner of one eye and slowly tricked down his cheek. Jackie jumped up, moving around the table and sat next to him, embracing him around the shoulders in deep, caring silence. Ripley couldn't hold out any longer, and all the anguish flooded out like a breaking Dam. His shoulders heaved up and down, his breathing became laboured, and the tears flowed like a river down his face. Jackie just pulled him closer, resting his head on her shoulder.

They held on to each other for what seemed like an eternity. Finally, Ripley was able to get himself under control. He sat back, wiped his face with the sleeve of his shirt, and looked gratefully into Jackie's eyes, giving her a hesitant smile. "I'm not sure what to do." His voice cracked. "It looks like Tommy might really be the guy we're after. I still can't believe it"

Jackie handed him a kleenex. "Don't jump to conclusions just yet," she responded quietly. "The answer to this problem may lead in other directions. For instance, what if the blood was stolen from a blood bank where your son or ex recently made a donation? A smart criminal could have done this to lead investigators off the track. There could be other explanations as well."

"Long shot." Faint hope began to well up in Ripley's chest. "Yeah, maybe." He smiled hesitantly.

Bald-headed Randall with his round face, heavily muscled arms, and salt and pepper goatee, wiped the bar with a soiled, damp cloth. He wasn't actually Tommy's partner as Ripley had been led to believe. He was really just a loyal flunky; he wasn't too swift, but did whatever he was told. Tommy believed Randall would do anything for him, even die, if necessary.

Unbeknownst to his dad, Tommy was using the bar as a front for his lucrative drug business. He was a user himself, but managed to keep it under control enough to keep the business up and running. The money was too good for him to screw it up. The cartel that supplied him was pleased that his distribution network was one of the best in the city. Tommy always managed to put up a front as a successful, hard-working businessman.

So far, so good.

Tommy entered in a rush, slamming the door behind him. "Hey buddy," he said, looking Randall in the eye, beckoning him to follow. "We need to chat in the office." He scanned the bar, seeing it was empty.

"Okay, Boss." Randall put the rag under the bar and followed Tommy to the back room. "What's up?" he queried, closing the door behind him. He grabbed a beat-up chair and straddled it backwards. Tommy circled the desk and slumped into his creaky office chair. "Dad is snooping around, asking about my whereabouts, and I don't think he believes what I told him. I worked hard to earn his trust after the accident, even helped him to learn sign language and lip reading. He's so trusting..."

Tommy felt a wave of emotion: love, sadness, guilt.

"What's different now?" Randall looked puzzled.

"Apparently he thinks I was in the hospital snooping around when all that hullabaloo went down with that guy, you know, the weird crimes goin' on. Maybe he thinks I'm the killer," Tommy snorted. "Can you believe that?"

"No boss, not you." Randall grinned weakly, his gold front tooth shining out from between his lips.

"I need you to be my alibi if the damn cops come around asking questions. Yesterday, you were upstairs in my apartment helping me do the books, right?"

"I wasn't there," Randall knit his bushy brows, confused. "I was here working. The bar usually opens for business about four in the afternoon, but I spent the early part of the day cleaning and polishing, and sorting out the supplies."

"No. You were in my apartment helping me do the books," Tommy said, glaring at Randall, his pale blue, washed-out eyes blazing.

Randal finally caught on and grinned sheepishly. "Ah, right, Boss, now I remember. We were at your place working on the books. You couldn't have been at the hospital. Were you there?"

"No, Randall." Tommy sighed. "I wasn't there, but we need to make sure the cops don't start looking any deeper into our operations."

"I get you, Boss. I'll do my best."

"Thanks, buddy." Tommy got up and patted Randall on the back. "I'm counting on you. Gotta go now. See you later today. Make this bar pop."

Just as Tommy was about to open the main door to the street, it crashed open and Sutherland stormed in. Tommy put on a big phony smile. "Hi there Mr. Sutherland," he said, extending his hand. "Have you come to wet your whistle?"

"Tommy," Sutherland growled, ignoring the hand and glaring at him. "I'm following up on an investigation. I have a few questions."

"For me? I didn't do anything. Ask away."

"Not here," Sutherland retorted, glancing over at Randall. "In your office. This is private"

"My dad already asked questions. Why are you here? I don't have to answer anything."

"Yes you do," Sutherland came back. "Either here in a private room, or down at headquarters. Your choice."

"I don't see why, when my dad already questioned me. Maybe I should get a lawyer." His voice, to his chagrin, took on a whiney tone.

"Your call," Sutherland replied. "Look Tommy," Sutherland responded, softening his voice a little, "It's our job to be thorough. Just a few questions. Have you got an office or something?"

Tommy pointed to the back and sighed. "Follow me." He winked at Randall as he passed him and headed to the back. Randall pretended he didn't notice, and polished harder.

Settling into the chair behind his desk as Sutherland closed the door, Tommy pointed at the other chair which still was sitting backwards. "Grab a seat," Tommy said. Sutherland reversed it, sat, and pulled out a notepad.

"So, what do you want to know? Is this about the damn hospital again? I told dad where I was at that time."

"Yeah," Sutherland responded. "You said you were upstairs in your apartment working on your books. Can you prove it?"

"Look," Tommy responded, feeling edgy. "I already told dad that Randall was with me. He often helps me when I work on the books. It helps speed up that boring part of my business."

"Randall's that bald jerk at the bar?" Sutherland hooked his thumb over his shoulder at the door.

Tommy's temper flared, and his face reddened. "He's not a jerk!" He stood, clenching his fists angrily.

"Sit the fuck down," Sutherland gestured. "Let's try this again. Is that gentleman at the bar Randall?"

"Yes he is," Tommy retorted sullenly, tensely settling back in his chair.

"Well, here's what's going to happen. You go get him and bring him in here. Then you go out to the bar and leave us here to talk."

Tommy hesitated. "I'd like to be in the room when you give him the heavy-handed cop grilling."

"Not on your life. I need to talk to him alone."

Frustration flowered on Tommy's face as he sulked out the door, but he returned a minute later with Randall in tow. "Took you long enough." Sutherland's piercing eyes glared daggers at him. "Close the door on your way out."

Tommy pulled the door shut sharply. Sutherland turned to Randall. "Sit," he said, pointing at Tommy's Chair. Randall looked sullen, but meekly obeyed.

"How can I help you, detective?" His eyes skated around, not quite meeting Sutherland's.

"I need to establish your whereabouts when the crimes at the hospital were committed."

"What crimes?" Randall looked mystified.

THROUGH NUMEROUS QUESTIONS, RANDALL STUCK TO HIS guns, insisting he was with Tommy working on the business books. Sutherland couldn't find any cracks in his testimony, but somehow felt Randall wasn't bright enough to do the kind of book work needed to run a business. Sighing, he finally gave up, thanking Randall for his help and headed out the door. As he passed the bar, Tommy grinned at him. "Have a nice day, Mr. Sutherland. Hope you catch the bad guy." His voice had a slight tone of sarcasm.

Sutherland stomped out the door and headed back to the office. *Looks like we're back to square one.* As much as he didn't want it to be, Tommy's alibi seemed legit, and an alibi was a hard piece of evidence to dismiss. *So how could there be a familial match? Sarah?* Sutherland shook his head as he weaved through traffic. *No, not possible.* Another vague possibility kept swirling around his head, but he just shook it off. Not even worth considering.

His cell phone buzzed. A text. It was Ripley.

Dale.

It's Sarah.

CHAPTER 10

His head swam, and his latest booze binge threatened to expel itself on the tops of his loafers. Again. He felt like he was suspended in a tube of his own, floating in bloody water, senses dulled and darkened by the murky crimson sway. He felt seasick, floating there in his mind's eye, bobbing around like a duckling submerged just below the swell, having given up hope and simply allowed itself to be drowned by the drink. He couldn't look up from the top of those loafers, the landing pad for his next projectile expulsion. He knew they were moving all around him. He felt them, their stares, their unnecessarily hushed conversations, their pity. He lowered his head between his legs, squeezing his temples with his knees. His breath was shallow, small gulps of oxygen, his heart pumping the pressure of a firehose of blood through his trembling body.

A small cabin in the mountains, the smell of bitter dark roast hanging in the air, the sun shining off the smoky emerald sheen of the lake. The cry of a loon, the chatter of some manner of bucktoothed rodent scurrying about the trees. Peace. Happiness.

"You coming back to bed?"

She glides through the kitchen, drowning in a cozy flannel button-down shirt, legs bare and shining in the morning light. Her hair is tied up in a loose bun on top of her head, tendrils of strawberry blond brushing the pink rising in her cheeks. Lovely.

She turns her head and looks at him, right into him, her green eyes warm and beckoning. He follows. So many summer mornings like this, tucked away, nestled at the feet of the Three Sisters in Banff where they had met during a guided horseback ride...

"Mark?"

The wedding, knee deep in crisp snow sparkling like diamonds, the tip of her button nose red as Rudolph's glow in the cold shadow of the Sisters...

"Mark."

Her belly, swollen from the life within, the way she craved and devoured poutine with every fiber of her being.

"Mark!"

He came back. Away from the shadow of the mountains, away from her eyes and her hair and her smell. Back into the heat, the stench of diesel and kelp, the whine of boat engines cutting through the night.

"YOU WITH ME, RIPLEY?" SUTHERLAND SAID, GIVING RIPLEY a light slap on either cheek. "Buddy, what's wrong? What's happened?"

The scene was rather quiet. A handful of first responders—beat cops and EMS—were mingling about, waiting on the detectives. Sutherland had come in answer to Ripley's text, armed with only the address Ripley had sent him. Sutherland burned over as fast as was safely possible, and found a shit storm waiting for him.

"Sorry," Ripley said under his breath. "So sorry."

"Don't be," Sutherland said, half wondering if Mark was even speaking to him. "I'm glad you texted me. You don't need to respond on your own to these things. I mean, you shouldn't even have been called out. You're not on the badge anymore, and—"

"I wasn't called, Dale."

Sutherland stiffened. *He called me Dale.*

"Well then, how did you—"

"I was here."

Ripley promptly dropped to his knees onto the muddy gravel, heaved off to the side, then drove his forehead down into the rocky ground. A few nearby officers reached for him, but he shoved them off, opting instead to leave his face half-submerged in the muck.

The world slowed. Sutherland watched the people tending to Mark, the red and blue lights dancing in the trees, the open door of the building that allowed a yellow carpet of light to roll out down the steps, inviting the masses inside. Sutherland followed the carpet of light onwards and upwards, his feet carrying him on autopilot through the doors of the fish packing plant.

It was overwhelming, the smell of fuel and fish, brine and body odour. The airless warehouse was more often than not full of burly men who sweat and toiled, heaving and tossing around the spoils of the sea, processing for weight and quality the day's catch off the Pacific. All manner of ocean fauna passed through the building: bass, halibut, cod, salmon. The place smelled like all of them combined, topped with the fresh stench of kelp and sea water. Sutherland pushed a gloved hand across his nose, opting for the smell of latex over the ocean's bounty. He moved around steel processing tables heaped with fish but vacant of staff. The room had been cleared of all two-legged creatures so law enforcement could lock down the scene.

Further back he went, past tanks, machines he couldn't fathom the use of, and blood-soaked cutting floors.

Great. Should be no problem to collect blood evidence here.

In the depths of the warehouse, in a central area with heavily sealed doors and no windows, was the chill he had been looking for. Figuratively. Literally.

As the freezer door shut behind him, his muscles immediately tensed; partially from the cold, partially from the ominous expectation that swelled in his throat. He wrapped his jacket tighter around his body and hunched his shoulders to his ears.

"Has to be this cold?" Sutherland asked a nearby CSI.

"Yeah," the CSI said. "We gotta preserve everything, and that means maintaining the conditions. If we let her melt…"

Sutherland held up his hand to stop him from talking. A rush of heat throbbed on his face.

Let her melt…

He saw her. He had seen her when the CSI was speaking, but what he was looking at didn't register until moments later. Long moments, filled with grief, confusion, anger, guilt…

Sarah. She was just as stunning in death as she had been in life. Now, though, dead as a doornail, she was a piece of art. She was laid out in a cube of ice, suspended in frozen water as clear as crystal. Her red hair coiled every which way like fiery snakes, her nipples covered modestly by tendrils of her ginger locks. Her skin shone white as the driven snow and her eyes were hollow and grey, lifeless and without emotion.

Was she afraid? Upset? Was she at peace when she drew her last breath?

He would never know. And her face wasn't any indication, frozen in seeming apathy under a foot of solid ice.

"How..." Sutherland trailed off before he could finish his thought.

"We aren't sure. We'll know more once we get her out of there, but we think that a bottom layer of liquid was frozen, her body placed on top, and the rest of the liquid added before whatever mold was removed. Gives the appearance of her floating in the center of the ice."

"There's no blood," Sutherland noted.

"Nope. Two possibilities. First is that she died without a wound. Like no gunshot or stab or nothing. Poisoning, maybe, or her heart gave out. Something like that. No matter. I'd wager that's not it."

Sutherland cocked his head. "You find a cause of death?"

"Nope. But there should be blood."

The CSI tapped the ice block, indicating towards Sarah's hand. Sutherland moved in, his face close enough to fog the ice.

Her fingers, those slender, pale fingers that were touched with a dusting of freckles. Fingers that Sutherland had seen so many times, weaved through Mark's meaty hands or wrapped around Tommy's dirty little fingers. Gone. Hacked off right at the knuckle, leaving an open cut of bone and flesh that had been neatly cauterized before stilling her hands in the ice.

"Second possibility," the CSI continued, "is that she was killed elsewhere, cleaned up, and put in the ice once the blood was gone. The water is crystal clear, so there couldn't have been much left on her or comin' out of her."

Sutherland grimaced as he thought of the killing floor in the other room.

"We've thought of that," the CSI said, seemingly reading Sutherland's mind. "Don't worry. The guys are lifting every bit of blood they can find, regardless of whether or not it's swimming in scales."

Sutherland flashed a hot and hostile look towards the CSI who dared to let a corner of his mouth upturn at his insensitive pun. The CSI nodded curtly at Sutherland, then took his leave, giving Sutherland some time and space to process the surroundings. Sutherland stepped towards the giant cube of ice, towards Sarah, and all he could see was Mark. His former partner, a man who had once been his best friend, a man who held a piece of his heart, no matter how far away he drifted. Sutherland looked into the cold, dead face of Mark's ex-wife, and saw Mark's death there as well.

"Oh Mark," Sutherland said. He looking over Sarah's face, and in her deathly stare was a plethora of images of the past. "This will be your end, I fear. And I thought you had already crashed at rock bottom."

Sutherland felt a pain in his chest as he thought of his friend, of Tommy, and the familiar corpse before him. Another rush of heat drove him to his knees, and despair and guilt threatened to drown him and freeze him in an ice block of his own.

"Oh God. What have I done?"

He paced the room, worrying his fingers over his hair and scratching at his head.

"Not part of the plan. A deviation, not outlined, not calculated. It's all wrong,. So wrong. And her. *Her*?!"

He brought his fists up to his temples, pounding himself on either side of the head until his ears were ringing, then he sat in the rolling chair and steadied his breath. His heartbeat. His sweat turned cool, and his twittering digits stilled. Calm restored.

"Okay. Okay. Can't be that bad. I mean, aside from the fact she's gone, everything else can't be that bad, right?"

He reached over and took the remote off the table, flicking on the television with a soft crackle. He sifted impatiently through the guide, finally arriving on the local news channel. His finger hovered over the select key, not sure if he wanted to know that *they* knew, but he had to. He would soon enough, regardless of whether he pressed that button. So down it went.

Nothing yet. Local robbery, book festival at the park, rock concert bringing in record numbers over the weekend...

Then...

A woman in a blue suit, trademark journalist din to her voice, with an aerial video of a warehouse on the water surround by all manner of emergency vehicles.

A gruesome discovery this evening. A woman was found murdered and stored at a local fish processing plant. An employee entering the freezer came across the chilling scene...

His ears rang and his eyes blurred with tears.

Could it be her? Really? There?

The victim has been identified, but her name withheld from the media until all members of her immediate family have been notified.

What in the ever-suffering fuck was I thinking? Stupid! Stupid!

His fists met his temples again, this time with more vigor and less control. In one particularity exuberant strike, he clipped the bridge of his nose, and a crack rattled his brain before a geyser of blood let loose across his bare chest and torso. He ran out the door and down the dark hallway to the bathroom where he finally let loose a stream of vomit that, thankfully, found a landing spot in the drain at his feet. He wavered for a moment on shaky legs before stepping into the shower.

Clear water curdled with crimson filth as he rinsed the blood off his pallid skin. He ground his nails into his legs, trying to loosen the foreign flesh from beneath his nails. Scraps of skin and hair traveled down his body into the drain below, and he wondered while he washed: *Is that mine? Is that hers?*

Once his skin was raw and cleansed, he shut the water off and sat down in the puddle that lingered on the shower floor. He swirled the water on the stained tile with his finger, focusing on nothing more than the sensation of the wet, the cold, the nothingness. And a hair. A single red hair, caught on the brushed nickel grate of his drain. A hair that screamed at him, screamed his name, his sins, his flaws, his faults. The hair... it knew. It knew what he had done, but not why he had done it. Knew not why its owner's time had been deemed to expire. He didn't know, either. Not really. On the surface, maybe, but ultimately it boiled down to him. Who he was and what he had become. So he sat, staring at that hair, and his body allowed him to grieve. Grieve her, grieve his innocence.

"Oh God. I'm sorry. So sorry," Tommy said on the breath of a sob.

CHAPTER 11

The front door buzzer rang insistently. Tommy had just finished dressing. After a full night's sleep, he was determined to get his act together. He knew he had killed his mother, but it was an accident. His mind reeled at the memories of the night before. Nobody would know he had been there. His head was throbbing and his gut still roiled in constant protest. Stabbing his finger on the intercom answer button, he took a deep breath and sighed impatiently. "What do you want?"

"Mr. Ripley? Thomas Ripley? It's the police. We need to talk."

Tommy's mind exploded in agony.

They found her, and me.

Letting go of the button, his heart raced so hard he thought it would burst out of his heaving chest. His stomach rumbled like he was about to spew his guts. For a moment he entertained the thought of running out the back, but he forced himself to settle down. Running was not an option. That would just solidify his guilt. He desperately knew he had to feign innocence. The demanding buzzer rang again. Pressing the button again, he said, as calmly as he could, "Just a moment, I'll be right down."

Taking deep breaths, trying to clear his jittery mind, Tommy made his way down the stairs to the front of the closed bar. Opening the door casually, as if he had all the time in the world, he raised his eyebrows in a questioning manner, to the two, young uniforms standing there. "Yes, officers? How can I help you?" He tried to hide his trembling hands, one behind his back, and the other holding tightly to the door.

One of the police officers, who looked like he'd just finished high school, sheepishly stepped forward. He looked hesitant and green around the gills. "Mr. Ripley, my name is officer Keith," he nodded at the other man, "and this is Officer Huckabay. May we come in?"

"Sure." Tommy stepped back and held the door open. "Grab a bar stool." He quickly slipped behind the bar, resting his hands firmly on the polished oak surface so they wouldn't shake. "What's this all about? Did I run a stop sign or something?" He tried to grin in amusement, but it came off as a grimace.

"We prefer to stand, Sir." The men removed their hats. Officer Keith took a deep breath and launched right into it. "Mr. Ripley, we're very sorry to inform you that your mother is deceased, and it looks like a homicide."

Tommy had assumed that, but hadn't known for sure. It felt like a knife through the chest, the thought of his mother gone.

"We're unable to tell you more at this time since the investigation is just underway. We just wanted you to know before her name is released to the public. I'm sure you'll know more soon. The investigators will need to talk to you."

Tommy succeeded in looking surprised and shocked at the same time. "Dead?" He allowed his tears to flow. "What? How?" He felt safe in bringing his trembling hands to his face now. "What happened? Where is she?" he blurted, trying to show desperate shock.

"Sir. Perhaps you should sit down.," Officer Huckabay said, voice soft. "This must be a tremendous blow for you. Would you like us to call your father?"

Angrily, Tommy shot back with a vicious look. "No! I'm fine. Just tell me where she is and what happened. He slammed his hands on the bar causing the officers to jolt back on their heels.

"Sir, we can't tell you much right now. All we know is that she was found dead at the Oceanside Fish Plant. She's being transported to police headquarters as soon as the forensics are complete."

"Oceanside Fish Plant?" Tommy's eyes widened in total, unfeigned surprise. His mind reeled. All he could remember is being in her house. *What the Hell is going on?*

"Sir," officer Keith said, sympathetically, "we have to leave now. Are you sure you'll be okay? You sure we can't call Mark for you?"

"I'm okay," Tommy uttered in a confused voice before leading them to the door. He let them out, then locked the door behind them.

Am I going crazy?

All he remembered was his rage which resulted in his mom being killed accidentally. Then he'd run from her house. That's it. Feeling sick and shaky, he headed back upstairs.

Back in his apartment, Tommy sat at the small kitchen table putting his hammering head in his hands.

Should I tell the truth when the investigators come back? What's this about a fish processing plant? He hesitated, thoroughly bewildered. *Something's wrong here!*

He forced his thoughts back to when he entered his mother's house and played the scene over and over through his mind. Maybe he *was* going crazy. Maybe he did move his mother to the fish plant. But why? He didn't even know where the fish plant was.

THE PREVIOUS EVENING...

"What are you doing here? I thought you said you'd never darken my door again." Sarah gave him a scornful stare. She still looked great for a middle-aged woman, but the expression on her face gave her a certain ugliness to Tommy's penetrating eyes.

"Come on, Ma," Tommy said, agitated, as he pushed through the door. "I haven't seen you in a long time. Just wanted to see how you're doing."

"Sure." She started crying, angry. "Got your hand out for some cash? Can't afford to buy your dope today?"

Anger coursed through Tommy's body like a wild banshee. "I'm clean, Ma! Haven't done drugs in months!" He realized his voice had whiny tone to it. He hated that. It made him look weak.

"Right," Sarah snapped. "You're not off drugs, I can see it in your face! You're still using, and probably pushing, too. You can't fool me! What a pair. You, a druggie, and your Dad an alcoholic. How did we get here?"

Extreme anger exploded in Tommy's brain. "How did we get here? Really, Mom?" He screamed and launched himself at her, giving her a solid push. Sarah stumbled back in surprise and fell backwards. She tried to grab Tommy, but her fingers just brushed the front of his shirt. Her head caught the corner of the dining room table with a loud crunch, and she slumped to the floor. Tommy stopped and stared at her, his heart rapidly beating and his chest heaving with short, gasping breaths. Through the sudden silence, all he could hear was his thumping heart.

Kneeling, his anger dispersed, and replaced by dread and extreme guilt. He slapped her face. "Ma, wake up!" Nothing. He tried again. She didn't even twitch

No! NO!

Tommy panicked. Leaping up, he tore out the door.

A FEW MINUTES LATER, LOOKING THROUGH THE WINDOW OF the house, his mood changed to one of supreme amusement. Gleefully, he grinned.

You whore. Got what you deserve.

He'd already begun preparations for his next creation. He's taken a little side trip after learning about his new friend Ripley's wifey wife. He had to come check it out. Now his new creation could wait while he played with this one.

She won't be completely without use. A message, she will be.

He hugged the wall as a car screamed past, tires burning rubber and throwing dense smoke. Then a deathly quiet descended over the scene. No one in the neighbourhood seemed to react to the sounds. Everything returned to normal, just like nothing happened.

Turning back to the window, he studied her, sprawled awkwardly on the floor by the dining room table.

Dead as a pretty little doornail.

He chuckled. Grasping the window ledge, he raised himself up and quickly entered the open door. Quietly closing it behind him, he took a pair of latex rubber gloves from his pocket.

Always be prepared!

He chuckled at his own genius, then knelt down beside the woman and held two fingers to her neck.

A pulse! She's not dead!

The freezer truck belonged to the fish processing plant on the pier. He'd borrowed it for his next project—a simple message rather than creation—but this would work just fine.

This is perfect! Yes indeed! He looked at the unconscious woman. *Gotta get to work before the bitch wakes up!*

Quickly leaving through the front door, he ran to the truck, fired it up, and carefully backed it into the driveway so it almost touched the stairs to the front door. Exiting the truck, he looked casually around to make sure there were no curious onlookers. Everything was quiet and empty. He grinned, a flood of excitement coursing through his body, and quietly let himself back in the house. He knelt beside the woman, preparing to lift her when suddenly she moved! Turning her head toward him, she looked at him in a dazed, angry, shock. "Why in Hell did you do that, Tommy! You're crazy!" She stared at him, her eyes suddenly uncertain. "What the fuck's going on?" She tried to struggle to her feet.

He firmly pushed her back down. "Now, now, mother. You're just a little woozy. Just rest there a bit and I'll get a cool cloth for you head."

Sarah stopped resisting and lay quietly, studying him, terror in her eyes. He could see she didn't quite know what to make of him, so he just grabbed her hair and slammed her head to the floor with a hard crunch. Her eyes fluttered, and she lay quietly, lapsing back into unconsciousness. *That should keep you still for a while, little lady.* He chortled as he returned to the truck to get his duffle bag of special equipment. He'd been saving it just for an occasion like this.

Kneeling back down beside her, he took out his cleaver and his blow torch. Then he removed a small case with a loaded syringe. Slipping the needle carefully in her arm, he depressed the plunger and sent her off to dreamland. *That should hold her until she's done.* He grinned at the perfection of his planning. Carefully and precisely, he pushed her left hand flat to the floor and chopped each finger with the razor-sharp cleaver, quickly cauterizing them with the blow torch to avoid too much blood loss.

Ripley, you're going to have fun trying to figure this one out!

After a few minutes of meticulous work with a tiny, homemade tool, he stood and admired his work.

Perfect! A stunning distraction and apt punishment.

He gathered the finger tips, placed them in a small plastic bag, and closed it with a twist tie. Then he then went to the truck and opened the back.

Taking another look around to ensure he was unobserved, he went back in the house and stripped the woman naked before putting her inside the vehicle, first making sure no one could see them. Once inside, he carefully placed her in a mold partially filled with ice. He arranged her body in a graceful pose, covering her nipples with strands of her hair.

There you go, my little beauty. Time for you to go to the long sleep goodnight.

He smiled and giggled at his wit. He took the small plastic bag with the finger tips in it and placed it carefully under the small of her back so it could not be seen from above.

Then he checked the streets and surrounding houses

again. All was quiet. Taking a garden hose from the truck, he found a tap, hooked it up, and quickly brought it into the truck, placing the end carefully into the metal box. Turning the water on, he watched in fascination as the cold clear liquid crept slowly up and over the sleeping lady. When it reached her mouth and nose, she started to drown, which caused some jerking movement and gagging. He gently held her down till it was over. Once everything was quiet and the water had filled the box, he shut it down, then adjusted the body to his liking.

Damn, that water's cold!

Standing back, he admired his work for a moment, and made a few more adjustments before leaving, closing the door, and making sure the freezer controls were at their highest setting.

As he walked up the steps to the door to finish cleaning up, he heard a voice behind him. "Are you moving?" A little old lady with a cane and a pill-box hat was looking at him questioningly, with a big smile on her face. She obviously didn't realize this was a freezer truck, and not a moving van. "I always admired that house. But I've never been inside. Is it up for sale?"

He thought quickly, then flashed her the biggest smile he could, his mind racing with ideas. "Why, yes, madam. It will be soon. Would you like a little sneak peek before I close it up?"

"Absolutely," she grinned happily. "Wait till Harry

hears about this. He always wanted a place like this." She tapped her cane enthusiastically as she came past the truck and up the steps. He followed her inside and closed the door. Staring at the scattered clothes and smeared blood on the floor, she turned suddenly, a look of terror on her face. Before she could move or open her mouth, his fist crashed into the side of her head, knocking her to the floor.

Nosey Bitch!

He stomped hard on the side of her neck and her head until he was sure she was dead. He felt her pulse, just to make sure, then he dragged her by her feet into the bathroom. The cleanup took no time at all. Once he had completed everything, he settled on to the couch to watch a little TV until the ice had set.

He was exhausted, but happy. Before he knew it, he was fast asleep, with wild, happy dreams racing though his head. It was hours later that he awoke, the faint sounds of traffic luring him awake. Looking at his watch, he was sure enough time had passed to solidify his masterpiece. He headed out again, making sure he was unobserved. The case was frozen solid and the little lady looked like a beautiful statue right in the middle. Pleased with his work, He was on his way to the Oceanside Fish Processing Plant, which he knew was closed. It was Sunday night, but he had a key. He grinned to himself as he thought of his excellent planning. He had often delivered fish to that plant, so absconding with a spare key was a piece of cake.

He pulled in front of a huge overhead door. The rank odour of all kinds of fish surrounded him as he let himself in by a small side door and turned on the lights. He knew from previous visits that the plant had no security system.

All the better for me!

Opening the overhead door, he returned to the truck and drove it into the silent, foul-smelling interior, and backed up to the sealed doors of the large walk-in freezer. Using a nearby forklift, he was able to remove the ice-filled case and lower it carefully to the floor. The metal case had removable sides with rubberized seals. All he had to do was apply a little heat to loosen the ice, then he could remove the panels. Using his trusty blow torch, the ice was soon free from the metal. He lowered the sides and end pieces, leaving a beautiful, clear block of ice. He stood still for a moment, admiring his work and the perfect image inside.

Returning to the fork lift, he carefully raised the block of ice and trundled it into the huge freezer room. He chose the perfect place to leave it and lowered it gently into place. Then he backed out and sealed the freezer room door tight. He gathered up his tools and the metal panels, and returned them to the truck. Within a few minutes, he was on his was home, satisfaction gleaming on his face.

A good day's work!

He smiled and turned on Emmy Lou Harris, his favourite singer.

CHAPTER 12

Sighing deeply, Ripley rose to his feet, brushed himself off, and wiped off his face. It was time to get his act together. Taking a deep breathe, his mind went back to the strange text.

Your life, the lies, on ice.

Attached to the odd line was the address of the fish processing plant. Without much thought, Ripley skidded out the door, still suffering from an alcohol-induced headache and stomach cramps.

Twenty minutes later, his Ford Skyliner screeched into the empty gravel parking lot of the plant. All was quiet and dark.

Of course. Today's Sunday, and it's nighttime.

Climbing slowly out of the car, Ripley looked around, searching for some reason to be there. Seeing nothing, he headed to the entrance door. Fearing the worst, he decided he couldn't wait; he had to get inside. Looking around desperately, he spotted a metal bar leaning against the wall. Within seconds, the window on the top half of the door was shattered and Ripley was inside.

Now what?

Ripley turned on the lights and stared at the metal tables lining the cavernous, foul-smelling room. The place was entirely empty except for a big forklift near what appeared to be a walk-in freezer. He could feel the vibration of the noisy freezer unit struggling to keep the interior cold. He moved cautiously to the heavy freezer door and pulled it open. Freezing cold temperature and an ice-cold fog tingled on his skin as he searched around for a light switch. Finally finding it, he turned the blackness to light, blinking his eyes to adjust to the sudden brightness. The freezer was large with shelving loaded with all manner of sea creatures lining all the walls. His attention was immediately drawn to the massive block of ice in the middle of the room. Something was inside it. Cautiously moving closer, he saw the body of a woman imbedded inside. He moved closer, and suddenly his heart dropped like a rock and his knees buckled.

Sarah! Oh God!

Scrambling over to the ice block, he stared at her calm, beautiful face and familiar red hair through the crystal-clear ice.

What have I done?

Ripley couldn't take it any more. He clawed his way to his feet and staggered, tears streaming down his face, out the door to the parking lot. His brain and his stomach was reeling as he messaged the cops. Then he fell to his knees and broke down completely, his shoulders heaving violently as burning bile spewed from his throat.

Sutherland.

Now, hours later, everyone was milling around, including Sutherland, who was inside the plant. Taking great gulps of air into his lungs and rubbing the mud off his forehead, Ripley headed back inside on unsteady legs. Anger swelled in his body like a rising flame.

This guy. This mad man is gonna pay.

Even though they had been separated for some time, he still loved Sarah, missing her like he missed his life before the explosion. He knew Sutherland would be personally affected as well. He crashed through the door and headed to the crowd.

Sutherland was just rising to his feet after examining the ice block. Tears began flowing down his face, and his nose was running. Ripley gently took his arm and handed him a tissue from his pocket. Refusing to look at the block of ice, he urged Sutherland out of the room and led him to a quiet area where they could talk. "Dale, I feel I can get through this, but I need you to get back in the game, too. We can't both be blubbering idiots. We've got work to do."

"I know," Sutherland choked out, vigorously wiping his nose and cheeks. "I can't believe it's Sarah. I just need a few minutes to get settled." His eyes turned dark. "The asshole who pulled this off is going to suffer if I ever get my hands on him!"

They both found some office chairs to settle on and quietly talked about Sarah and how she had been a major part of both their lives for so long. The forensic crew let them be, knowing they needed time.

Finally, they steeled themselves and headed back to the freezer. Sutherland brought Ripley up to date on what had been found so far. "The missing finger tips must be a God-damned message of some sort. We need to get this to the lab and let Dr. Fields check it out. This has gotta be our guy."

Ripley grimaced.

Sutherland signaled the waiting crew who had began the process of taking the ice block to the lab. Then they continued their forensic examination of the scene. Ripley joined Sutherland in his police cruiser for a few minutes. "We may be back to square one on this one," Sutherland mused, "but I'm still not sure about Tommy's alibi."

"You actually think Tommy could kill Sarah? His mother? That's nuts!" Ripley knew he was over-reacting because his confidence in Tommy had waned as well.

"All we can do now is get back to headquarters and examine the evidence we have. We also need to get over to Sarah's house and check it out."

"You're right. It's going to take some time to thaw out the block of ice, so let's get cleaned up, grab some snacks, and plan out our next moves. I'll dispatch some officers to Sarah's place to seal it off till we can get there.

Ripley shook his hand and looked him in the eye. "Thanks for supporting me through this, Dale. Even though you're an asshole, sometimes."

Ripley headed to his Skyliner and followed Sutherland to police headquarters. He felt like he'd been dragged through a rat hole snd left for dead.

RIPLEY KNEW THE ICE BLOCK AND FORENSIC EXAMINATION would take some time, so he and Sutherland took some time to get cleaned up, had a bite to eat, and filled up on hot, streaming coffee. Feeling a little less like zombies, they rode together in Sutherland's cruiser to Sarah's home, both brooding in silence. Thoughts of Sarah enveloped their thoughts in different ways. They knew the location like the back's of their hands. The officers that had been sent there earlier were ordered not to enter, just to seal the place up and wait. So when they arrived, yellow tape had been tied off around the property, and the officers were fending off curious onlookers.

"Put these on," Sutherland said, tossing Ripley a pair of latex gloves and boot covers. Once they were ready, they entered though the unlocked front door and silently viewed the familiar interior. They found a tidy, clean room with no sign of turmoil of any kind. Careful not to disturb anything, they began to search through the deathly still house. Ripley choked up at the memories of the place that had been his home for many years. Separating, Ripley went through the living and dining room to the kitchen while Sutherland headed down the hall to the bedrooms and the bath.

So many meals he had eaten at that table, Tommy's highchair set at one end. They had bought the small bungalow a year before they had married when it had been a buyers market. It wasn't worth much now, but Ripley would have paid a hefty sum to stay within its walls. Even now, after what happened to Sarah, he wished he could be back there again, smelling meals in his kitchen, watching television in his living room, and hearing the sound of Tommy's laughter ringing through the halls.

Suddenly, Ripley was aware of rapid vibrations from someone running nearby. Sutherland rushed in and grabbed Ripley by the arm, turning his head toward him.

"The bathroom."

Together they entered the room in question and stared at the dead woman piled into the bathtub. There was no question she was dead, her head obviously crushed.

Sutherland looked at Ripley. "Do you know who this is?

Ripley leaned over to feel for a pulse just in case, but shook his head.

"Mrs. Steinham. She and her husband, Harry, live just down the street."

"Call it in," Sutherland said to a nearby lackey. "Looks like we have a double homicide."

"Wrong place, wrong time, I imagine," Mark said, stroking her wrinkled cheek.

The forensic team arrived shortly after, combing the scene for evidence. Once the processing was well under-way, Sutherland and Ripley headed back to headquarters.

CHAPTER 13

"You okay?"

Jackie Field's eyes were still stunning, despite her obvious worry. She lifted a gloved hand, moving it towards Ripley's shoulder, but let it drop to her side instead.

Ripley responded by nervously running his fingers through his dark hair.

The note was laid out in front of him on the stainless steel counter. Same handwriting, same scratches of crimson.

Watch them born

Watch them bleed

Created from

Desperate need

Ripley stared at the note, rearranging the words in his

head, trying to pick out code or meaning, but the notes all jumbled together—a dissonant song.

"I'm not sure there's any sense to be found there, Mark."

"There's something. There's a reason for all of this."

"Not necessarily."

Ripley breathed deep and closed his eyes. "Okay. So what do we have with the body?" He opened his eyes and looked at Jackie's face.

"Eyes, ears, same as the other one. This one is missing a hand, but like they said at the scene, it's a hack job. Something done in anger. Hasty and crude. Fresh, too, when he went in the box. Confetti was stuck into the wound."

"Perp fought back?"

"Unlikely. Sedative in his system suggests that he was pretty gorked out. Probably couldn't even blink his eyes, even when he still had them."

"Huh. Odd that, then. Wonder why the hand got the chop."

"Mark, there's something else. Something about all of this. This isn't a novice doing this."

Jackie walked over to the body in the center of the room and pulled back the sheet. Ripley had seen his fair share of corpses, and was more troubled by those out in their natural setting—dump sites, car accidents, OD's. In the morgue, though, death was an easier death to swallow. A body here was expected, normal; a corpse in a morgue was no different from a piece of furniture.

But this body was something different.

Eyes mutilated, ears shredded, mouth a torn and gaping void where his tongue had once been. It was a level of brutality Ripley had never encountered, even more brutal than sewing a bomb into someone's belly.

"You're saying this is a doctor," Ripley said.

"I know it looks crude, but it's a fairly precise medical procedure. The way the eyes are removed, the missing bones in the ears."

"Bones?"

Fields went to her laptop and peeled off her gloves. After clicking through a few files, she came up with a diagram of the structure of the inner ear.

"The bony labyrinth of the inner ear? This has been completely removed. The malleus, incus, stapes, and all corresponding ducts. It was precise work, sharp cuts, removal with specially crafted instruments..."

Jesus fucking christ.

"Mark, a regular doctor would have difficulties with this kind of procedure."

"So a specialist of some kind?"

"A surgeon, probably."

"Okay. That gives me something to go on. I can look up surgeons in the area, educated or practicing—"

"Mark." With the gloves now off, Jackie was able to

offer her touch. She held Ripley's shoulders and moved close to his face. "This person could have come from anywhere. Any medical school, in or out of the country."

"Gotta take any lead we can."

"You need to take it easy, Mark."

Fields took Ripley's face in her hands and pressed her lips against his. Ripley flushed, waves of confused emotion, of want and sorrow, excitement and panic flowing through his body. He didn't pull away, though, fully tasting her before she took a step back.

"I care about you Mark."

He was speechless, his mind blank.

"Go," Fields said, giving him a little shove. "Do your thing."

THE GREEN LAMPS ON THE TABLES OF THE CITY ARCHIVES provided little overall illumination to the room as a whole. It was a library of sorts, a collection of records and books containing the history and statistics of the city and surrounding counties. Ripley riffled through papers and surfed microfiche, trying to find graduates around Tommy's age.

Why would I do that?

Because it looked like Tommy.

It wasn't Tommy.

Just someone who looked like him—his age, his size...

Graduation photos from various universities, medical programs, the surgical residency at the University of Alberta—Ripley reviewed them all one, two, three times, holding a magnifying glass over each and every face, trying to decide if it was his son's doppelgänger.

Or maybe...

No.

It's not Tommy.

Tommy was a good man. He had trouble as a youth, which Ripley attributed to the disruption to their lives from the explosion. It had been a tumultuous childhood for his son, full of a dying marriage and a father who refused to fully heal. While Ripley grieved the loss of his hearing, his son was supposed to be growing, a difficult feat that should have been fostered by attentive and compassionate parenting. Ripley's selfishness, combined with the consequential end of his marriage—a union he was lucky to have had—resulted in his son turning to substances rather than relationships for comfort. And as much as Ripley abhorred what drugs did to the young years of his son's adulthood, he hoped—in deep, dark hidden places of his mind—that the drugs provided some pleasure and respite from Tommy's grim reality.

Ripley pulled his cellphone out of his pocket and started Texting.

You busy? We should grab some grub.

Ripley hesitated, then typed some more.

No hidden agenda, no trouble. I just want to see you. To hang out. Promise.

After waiting ten minutes, Ripley was about to type in another message when a text from Tommy came through.

Sounds good, Dad. Golden Star? Couple hours?

Ripley smiled.

Sounds perfect.

After pouring over documents for the better part of an hour, Ripley tossed the white flag, considering his search to be dead. He gathered his belongings and headed to the door of the archive, looking at the painting of the surrounding prairies on the wall. Still life oil painting of canola fields, barns, a tractor...

Farm.

Ripley rolled an idea around his head as head as he headed out to go meet his son.

CHAPTER 14

Ripley had been going to the Golden Star for as long as he could remember; it was his favourite restaurant, aside from the Keg. They had amazing Chinese food—his favourites being the sweet and sour chicken and the ginger beef. Most of all, though, he loved being there with his family, Sarah sipping on wonton soup as Tommy rolled his chicken balls over the table.

It was like old times, Ripley chewing his ginger beef, Tommy pushing his chicken balls around his plate with a fork. But this time, Tommy had a beer in front of him. And there was no Sarah.

"Any leads?" Tommy asked.

In the recent past, Ripley would have assumed Tommy was coming down from a high. There was sweat forming on his son's brow and his hands were trembling. But now Ripley wasn't so sure if he was coming down, or just nervous. Or both.

"We have evidence," Ripley said, "but no direction yet. Lots of leads."

"Who would do that to Mom?"

As Tommy spoke, his words were marred by a slight quaver. Ripley felt a lump rise in his throat.

"Someone who didn't know her. No one who knew Sarah would have ever…"

They ate in silence for the next few minutes, neither wanting to speak. Speaking required looking at each other, and looking at each other would be the cause of bursting dams, tears on both sides. Ripley played out options in his mind: talking about the weather, about the bar, about Tommy's latest relationship. Nothing seemed appropriate. He had to tear off the bandage.

"Tommy," he said, setting down his fork. "I'm sorry."

Tommy stopped chewing and set his fork down beside his plate. After a moment and a few breaths, Tommy looked up at Mark. His eyes were wet with tears.

"For what?"

"For everything." Ripley cleared his throat. "After the accident… you needed me. Sarah needed me."

"Dad, you were hurt. Bad. You were healing."

"I was selfish."

"Your hearing—"

"Took some getting used to, yeah. I never have, really. Probably never will. But it's one sense. I had so much more than my hearing. I'm so much more than deaf. I should have been more for you."

Tommy went to respond, but closed his mouth shut into a tight, quivering line instead. He looked away, wiping his eyes with the heels of his hands.

"I love you, Dad. I'm sorry, too."

Ripley let the tears flow, streaming down his cheeks as he watched his son, now a man, a boy who had survived Ripley's trauma, and still had his whole life ahead of him. Ripley would stand by him, be the dad he needed.

"Dad, I'm not clean anymore."

"I know."

"I'm sorry."

"It's not the end of the world. We'll deal with it. Rehab, when you're ready. Small fish to fry."

"I... I've done bad things."

"We've all done bad things."

"I sell, Dad."

"I figured. We can get you out of that, too, if you want. It's more important you're clean. We can deal with the business later. I don't want to see you in jail—"

"Mom."

Ripley's stomach clenched. He pressed his palms against the table, bracing himself for Tommy's next words.

"Can I get you another drink, sir?"

The server stood over top of Tommy, motioning to his empty glass of beer.

"No. Thanks."

"And you—"

"No." The word came quicker and faster than Ripley intended. The server look stung, but slinked away with no further questions. Ripley let silence marinate the air. He was used to it—could resist its tension—but Tommy couldn't. Silence was an order to speak, to fill that space that hung in the air, both accusation and confession.

"Mom," Tommy repeated, sweat glistening under his nose. "I think... I don't know."

"Don't know what?"

"I didn't... I was mad. We fought, but I didn't... and the fish plant. I've never been there, Dad. I haven't."

Tommy broke down, his head plummeting into his hands, sobs shaking his body as diners at nearby tables stole glances. Ripley stood and moved to Tommy, wrapping his arms around his son. He felt sick for Tommy's torment, but more than that, he felt anger. And fear.

"Tommy?"

Tommy looked up at Ripley, his face soaked with tears.

"You fought with Mom?"

Tommy nodded.

"Just the other night?"

Another nod.

"When she..."

Tommy nodded, and a sob barked out of his mouth. The tears flowed again, this time with more vigor.

"Tommy, did you kill Sarah?"

Though Ripley had been immersed in silence for many years, this new silence was deafening, a rock dropped on his soul. Tommy considered his answer, or the question, everything—Mark wasn't sure what. After an uncomfortably long lack of response, Tommy looked up at his father, but still couldn't form a word. Any word. Instead, he gave a weak shrug, and lost control again. He stood up, his body heaving with sobs, and rushed to the exit.

Ripley let him go. He would have to act soon—he was concerned Tommy would do something desperate—but his head was spinning. Turn in his son? Even investigate his son?

Then again, Tommy said he didn't know. He didn't know if he did it.

Ripley picked up his phone and stabbed the screen with a frantic finger.

Tommy. I know you're upset, but it's okay. I'm doing anything, I'm not speaking to anyone. I'd like to talk to you about what happened. About the fight with Mom. I will help you, I just need to know what happened. I don't think you have a clear picture, but we can sort this out. Together.

Send.

Then Ripley typed another message.

Tommy, I'm not a cop anymore. I'm not questioning you or taking you in. Just a dad and son. A talk. Promise.

Send.

Ripley's finger hovered over the screen, wanting to type another message, to send his heart straight to Tommy, but he backed off. He didn't want to pressure Tommy or scare him off even more.

"Package up the rest of your food, sir?"

The waitress stood a meter away from the table, looking absolutely terrified.

"Yes, please. I'm sorry, it was wonderful. We just…"

Ripley trailed off, not knowing what up to say. A few minutes later, he was standing outside the restaurant, foil containers in hand, wondering what he was going to do.

Like strutting across bales of cotton, he bounced down the street, happy as a pig in shit. He strutted into A&W, not giving a solitary fuck about the fat and calories—he was healthy as a horse and deserved some comfort food. And the treat would also help lift the mood of his latest creation.

"Teen burger, Mozza burger, two fries, and two root beers, if you please."

The cashier punched in the order, looking uneasily over the counter at his customer. After a few minutes, he was back on the street, strolling towards his lab with food in his hand. As he passed a park, he spied an empty table and sat down to eat his lunch.

"No good eating with the rodent!" He laughed quietly

to himself. A few people sitting on nearby benches moved away.

He chewed and drank, watching people going to and fro, young and old, holding briefcases or shopping bags or hands of loved ones. On the surface, it was beautiful, but that was just make-up; it was a homely face spackled with layers of foundations and rouge and lipstick.

No, he thought. *Not homely. Downright ugly. Hideous.*

Greedy, judgmental, hateful.

The lot of you.

He watched as people passed, looking at each other, speaking with each other. Each tainted by the others hate, their inherited prejudice. Cellphones delivered messages of intolerance, of poisoned rhetoric, tainted news and harmful groupthink that would sink the world.

Feral lemmings.

He couldn't look at them anymore, the ants shuffling around, thinking with other people's brains, products of the opinions of others.

Frustration replacing gluttony, he threw the remainder of his burger in a nearby bin and charged towards home to his lab where his creation awaited him.

"... AND THEY WERE EVERYWHERE, NATTERING TO EACH other, bitching about things they hadn't felt or seen or heard firsthand. They couldn't give one single furious fuck about facts or decency or positivity."

He put the burger up to his creation's mouth, pressing the greasy patty against his lips. The creation took a large bite, ravenous for food.

"Looks like someone is on the mend," he said, a wide, toothy smile stretching across his face.

He continued to feed the creation his burger and fries until the boy turned his head away, sated. He placed the straw in the creation's mouth so he could suck up the fluid.

"That's right. You'll be back to normal soon. Well, your new normal. A better normal."

Once every bit of food and drink had been consumed, he rolled his chair away from the table and threw the trash in the bin.

"Let's get you cleaned up and go for a walk, shall we?"

After pulling on a pair of latex gloves he fetched from the sink, he washed the creation's face with a wet washcloth, cleaning away the sauce and cheese that had dribbled down his chin.

"Okay, let's do our hands in the bathroom. After you do your business, of course."

He took the creation's hands and gently pulled him off the bed. The boy stood in one spot, wavering on his feet. He guided the boy a few steps then let go, backing towards the door of the lab. The boy's feet stopped.

"No no. Keep coming."

He took the boy's hands again and led him a few more steps. When he stopped, the boy stopped. He looked at the boy and stomped his feet hard on the ground four times. The boy tilted his head. He took the boy by the hand and stomped his foot four times before taking a few steps. He repeated this process several times, holding the boy's hands while they walked. When they reached the doorway to the hall, he dropped the boy's hands and walked to the end of the hall. Standing there, facing the boy, he stomped his feet. The boy tilted his head and didn't move. He could feel frustration rising in his belly as he watched the boy, his pale face, furrowed brow.

But then...

A step.

"Yes! Yes!"

He stomped on the floor again, and another step. Then another.

The boy keep walking until he reached him at the end of the hall. Thrilled, he gave the boy a firm pat on the back, causing the boy to jump. With a gentler hand, so as not to rattle the boy further, he led him into the bathroom and guided his hands to the toilet.

"Go," he said, touching the boy's hand to the seat several times. When the boy clued in and started pulling down his sweatpants, he turned to give the boy his privacy. When the boy had completed relieving himself and pulled him his pants, he led the boy to the sink where they went through the motions of hand washing.

Once the entire bathroom routine was complete, he led the boy back into the hall and placed his hand against the wall. The boy stood, more confident this time, and he pushed the boy softly on the back, steering him towards his room. The boy needed little encouragement, walking boldly towards the room until he crossed the threshold, made it across his room, and his shins touched his bed. The boy sat and exhaled heavily, and a smile teased across his lips.

A smile.

The boy hadn't smiled once, not since he'd taken him over a year before.

He ran to the boy, kneeling beside the bed and putting his hands on the boy's legs.

"We're doing it! We're really doing it! The other's didn't work—epic failures on their part, but you..."

He touched the boy's cheek, taking care not to touch the area near where his eyes used to be.

"You are an evolutionary miracle. The beginnings of a new, beautiful normal."

CHAPTER 16

The smell was still there, that same one hiding within the aroma of blood and death when Ripley had first stepped out of his vehicle not that long ago. Ripley knew what it was now. Standing in front of the veterinarian's office, staring at the yellow police tape that still hung over the doors, Ripley breathed deep, tasting that familiar and now identified smell.

Farm.

It had clicked in his brain when he was in the archives, staring at that oil painting. Inside the veterinarian's office, he had immediately identified the smell of blood—he had anticipated that. He knew the smell of dogs and cats, and possible rodents. But what he hadn't pinpointed right away was a faint scent of farm: hay, canola, livestock...

Ripley looked around at the other businesses, curious eyes looking back at the strange man with the scar across his face hovering around the mysterious scene. After making eye contact with one of the shopkeepers, Mark decided it was time to go for a chat. The little bell chimed as Ripley walked through the door of Farm Supply.

"G'day sir," the keeper sang out. He hustled behind the counter as soon as Ripley stepped through the door.

These folks must be spooked, a crime like that right here in their world.

"I work with the police department," Ripley said. A half truth. "My name's Mark Ripley."

"Judd here," the old man said, smile wide and honest.

"I'm just asking around about the incident that occurred here last week," Ripley said.

"Horrible thing, that. Every find the guy?"

"Getting close. Just tightening up a few leads. You see anything on that day? Or around that day?"

"Already spoke to the other officers..."

"Indulge me."

Judd looked Ripley up and down, lingering on the silver slice across his face. Either out of fear or pity, he decided to participate.

"Nothing much new," Judd said. "Same old customers, all the businesses, us and the vet. Only new folks I've seen was that couple that stopped in with their cat, smooshed by the missus backin' out her driveway. She was in too much of a rush, and the cat twern't very smart. Not a good combination."

"Anyone hit both businesses? Come here with a pet then head next door? Without a pet, even?"

Judd scratched the grey stubble on his face. "Can't say, really. Not always watchin' all the folks, but I suppose there coulda been a few shop hoppers. Maybe people gettin' farm supplies here, pet food there. Dunno."

"Okay. Any odd ducks? Customers that bought odd stuff?"

"Mostly regulars, people stoppin' in from the highway, needin' parts and stuff."

"Tires?"

"That, though we only have a few. We have a smattering of all sorts of stuff for fixin' machinery, doing lawns and gardens."

Judd's eyes scanned the shelves, trying to find answers amongst the feed and fertilizer.

He wants this put to bed as bad as I do. No one wants a beast on the loose.

"No, nothing unusual, just the usual. Weed killer, mousetraps are flying off the shelves right now. Those pesky vermin aren't partial to the extra developments, buildin' on their hidey holes in the fields..."

C'mon old man.

"Tools, parts... we can only be so big, jus' me and the missus running this place solo, so we don't always have what people need. Some of the locals dump off old junk 'round back, and people pick through those parts if we haven't anything shiny and packaged."

"Car parts?"

"Yep. And mowers, cars, quads… all sort of useless, dead stuff. I don't know nothin' about it, but it's of interest to some, mechanics and such, I suppose."

Steel.

"Anyone come in for lots of steel?"

"Car parts and such?"

"Useless parts, maybe? Odd parts?"

"Plenty. Johnny over at the car dealership, the guys at the airport towards the city. Even the county itself comes in from time to time."

Ripley was stumped. "Can I take a look out on your yard?"

"Yer welcome to poke around anywhere you please, young man! I want this rat captured bad as you do."

"I figured."

Judd led Ripley through the shop to the fenced yard behind. Ripley could tell that Judd was speaking to him —his hand flailing and shoulders rising and falling as he led the way—but Ripley had no idea what he was saying. Probably for the best. His head was already crammed full of thoughts.

The yard had a selection of new mowers and garden tools, plants, bags of mulch and dirt, and other assorted yard needs. Along the back fence, against the trees, was the steel graveyard—about a half dozen clunkers, rusted, doors askew, some old bicycle frames, riding and push mowers. Ripley wandered through the abandoned metal, peeking under hoods and looking towards the veterinarian clinic. A lump formed in his throat and he clenched his fists. An overwhelming urge to punch one of those cars washed over him. To punch it over and over again until his knuckles were bruised and busted and his pain bled out with the gushing blood.

A hand grasped his shoulder, jarring him away from his anger. He turned to face Judd, whose face was scrunched in worry.

"Ya in a daze, son? Hear what I said?"

Ripley sighed.

"Sorry," Ripley said, pointing at his ears. "Deaf".

Judd's expression softened. "Ah shit, sorry."

Ripley waved it off. "No worries. How could you know?"

"You hide it well."

Ripley hadn't thought of that. He never actively hid it, but there was nothing to see. Silent, blind suffering.

"I can read lips like I've been doing it my whole life."

"I dare say! Without a hiccup, sure! But don't be bashful. It ain't you, jus' somethin' you got."

Tears welled in Ripley's eyes. He was about to change the subject when Judd saved him the trouble.

"'Bout weird business," Judd said, hauling open the hood of an old Buick, "young buck does come in here once a month or so, picks up some general supplies—chicken feed, paper goods, weed n feed—but he always has a boo back here. I asks what he's looking for, and he's nonchalant, but pretty specific."

Judd pointed into the car, like Mark would know what was missing.

"Leaf spring. Got 'em in mid-century cars."

"What would someone use that part for?"

"Not the part. The steel. That big ol' spring is a good haul for someone seekin' scavenged steel."

"Scavenged steel. Useful for…"

"Forging new shit, tools and such. Not cost efficient, but cool if you like makin' your own stuff."

There it is.

"This young buck," Ripley said. "Did you get his name?"

"Naw, sorry. Possible he pays with a card, but I have no idea. Wouldn't be able to tell you when he was last in."

"Can you remember what he looks like?"

"Probably… my old noggin' ain't so good for stuff like that."

Ripley reached in his back pocket and pulled out his cell phone.

"Is it this guy?"

Ripley held up a picture of Tommy. Judd pulled his

glasses out of his shirt pocket and moved closer to the phone, squinting and studying the picture.

"Somethin' similar, yeah. Pretty close, I dare say."

Ripley's heart wedged in his throat. He shoved the phone back in his pocket.

"Who is he? Is it..." Judd wagged his finger at the vet clinic.

"Possibly. I sure hope not."

CHAPTER 17

"So where are we at?"

Ripley felt Sutherland's words, but didn't see the question. He had his head in his hands, trying to piece together the facts with his emotions.

"Mark."

Sutherland touched the top of Ripley's head. Ripley sat up and looked at the board in the conference room.

"Okay," Sutherland said. "Thanks for joining me."

"Fuck you."

"Indeed."

"So," Sutherland said, pointing to the board. "Vic one, floating in a fucking tube, goat bone through his ear and mutilated."

Ripley's eyes studied the pictures, blood swirling, a lava lamp of death.

"Vic two, confetti, mutilated but lived, then the killer finished the job in the hospital."

He studied the pictures, the body in the box, the oxygen tank...

"No," Ripley said. "He didn't intend for the victim to die. Initially. He was keeping him alive with the oxygen. Something changed after we got him."

"What changed?"

Ripley considered the scenario, the security footage in the hospital.

"He talked," Ripley said, more to himself than Sutherland. "That's why he cut out his tongue."

"But surely he must have known the guy would talk. I mean, fuck, Ripley! The guy was tortured!"

"So specific, though. Both victims."

"What of the old woman in Sarah's apartment? What about Sarah?"

Ripley winced at her name.

"Like I said, if Sarah was the target, the old woman was likely collateral damage. Wrong place wrong time."

Sutherland paused, fiddling with the files on the table.

"Go ahead," Ripley said. "We need to go through this."

Sutherland hesitated, but continued.

"Sarah struck her head on the corner of the table, but that didn't kill her. Cause of death was drowning."

"No mutilation."

"Just the fingers."

"Huh."

Ripley reached for a file and riffled through the papers.

"The fingers. Whore." He noticed that Sutherland was shifting nervously from foot to foot. He looked up, and saw the pen in his mouth, clenched between his teeth.

He's nervous. Why?

"The samples from the notes," Mark said. He noticed Sutherland grimace. "Let's review that."

"Not much to review."

"You think it's Tommy."

Sutherland said nothing. He stared at the file in Ripley's hand.

"I don't see Tommy doing this," Ripley said, closing the file. "I don't... I can't..."

Sutherland sat in the chair beside Ripley and held his hand. "Mark."

Ripley fought the impending tears, refusing to break down.

"Mark," Sutherland said. "It's not your fault. If this is Tommy, his action are his and his alone. He's a grown man with a mind of his own."

"I ruined his childhood, Dale."

"You did no such things. Kids are resilient—"

"I was an asshole. *Am* an asshole. I should have been there for him."

"You did the best you could. You were suffering, Mark. Still are."

"I can't. I refuse to believe this is Tommy. He's no saint, that's for sure, but a *killer*? And his mom? Not a chance."

Ripley said the words, trying to convince Sutherland, but also himself.

"Okay. Well where are we going next?"

Ripley stayed silent again.

Sutherland stood and moved back to the board. When he faced Ripley again, his look was less sympathetic.

"Don't do this, Ripley."

"Don't do what?"

"Pull away. Like you do."

"What are you talking about?"

"Floating away on your own, doing your thing. Without the force. Without me."

"I'm not on the force anymore, remember? They took that away from me when I lost my hearing." Ripley stood and pushed his chair into the table. "Lost my hearing, my job, my family... I'm pretty sure I can do whatever the fuck I please."

"Mark—"

"You have a case to solve. Have fun."

Ripley stormed out of the conference room, slamming the door behind him.

AFTER MARK STORMED OUT OF THE ROOM, SUTHERLAND stood and stared after him.

What a mess. What have I done?

The pictures on the board reached out for him, every printed word an accusation. The young man in the tube stared at him through empty sockets, boring into his soul. A printout of the security footage at the hospital was blown up and pinned beneath the picture of the confetti body. Sutherland moved in close to the picture, nose almost touching the grainy black and white print.

"Is that you?"

Very much like Ripley, Sutherland swiped the thought from his mind, turning his attention to the files on the table.

"So what are you up to, you sneaky bastard?"

Sutherland flipped through the files, trying to figure out what was going on in Mark's head. He flipped through interviews, forensics, witnesses. Nothing jumped out at him, though his mind kept wandering to the board, and the distorted security photo.

Sutherland picked up his phone and punched in a number.

"Hello. Yeah, I'm hanging in there."

Sutherland signed and rubbed his eyes.

"Look. It's time we had a talk."

CHAPTER 18

Canola fields whizzed by the window, golden yellow against the pink backdrop of the rising sun. Paper in hand, Ripley looked at the list, all but four of the names and addresses crossed off. Judd couldn't quite recall the details about the steel-scavenging stranger, but he did know that, from time to time, he was picking up corn and goat feed. Mark thought the perhaps he did that as a front, something to distract from the odd purchase of metal, but the guy would have picked something smaller, cheaper, and easier to dispose of. Judd also said that it wasn't the first time he had bought feed at the store.

Ripley surmised that this mystery man was buying supplies for a nearby farm where he either worked or lived. Judd gave him a list of customers who ran a farm that had either fowl or small livestock. Ripley wasn't confident that any of the people on the list would be associated with the guy—he probably didn't register under his name or the correct address—but Ripley had to go on something. The first seven stops had been a bust, but Ripley carried on to the eighth.

This farm was beautiful, secluded from the main road by a thick barrier of trees. Even more than that, the main road leading to the driveway was a lightly travelled gravel road, making the spot even more isolated. As Ripley rolled his Fairlane out in the open through the tunnel of trees, the farmhouse came into view. A two story white home with a porch that wrapped around the front and side of the house, it looked like something from a postcard. Coconut hair flower baskets hung from the porch, tendrils of trailing pansies in a bold array of whites, blues, and purples spilling over the sides. A wind chimed topped with a cardinal sang its tinkling song, the crystal hanging between the tubing sparkling in the morning sun.

As Ripley parked the car, a woman stood up from the garden, floral gardening gloves up to her elbows and knees stained with grass and dirt. She was older, perhaps a decade Ripley's senior, with lovely, long, lean body and thick blonde hair tied at the base of her neck in a loose plait.

Ripley stepped out of the car and sucked air deep into his belly.

There it is. That smell.

The woman was talking, but Ripley was too far away to make out what she was saying. Instead, he looked around the property, taking in all the smells, the sights, the feel of the air. There was livestock here, for sure, and the smell of the woods, fresh and piney. The driveway continued on past the house to a large red barn in the back.

The woman was close now, her step slowing, her expression communicating her concern for the lack of communication or reception from her new guest.

"I'm terribly sorry," Ripley said. "I know you were speaking to me, but you were too far away for me to make out what you were saying." Ripley pointed sheepishly to his ear. "I'm deaf."

Her face dropped, then morphed into a smile, and she held out a hand.

"Oh my stars, I am the one who should be offering apologies! Truth be told, I was cussin' you out when you didn't answer. I've had more than my share of solicitors out here, even though I'm off the beaten path."

Funny, that. Because I'm deaf, she doesn't see me as a solicitor. Or a threat.

"Mark Ripley," he said, holding out his hand.

"Camille Bowker." She clasped his hand, cupping the other overtop and giving it a squeeze. And to what do I owe the pleasure?"

She batted her full lashes and tucked a sprig of hair behind her ear.

Beautiful. Flirty.

Trouble.

I'm a... friend of the family. I mean, the family of one of those victims in that recent..."

"Oh gosh," she said, her hand coming up to her chest. "That messy business in town?"

"Yes," Ripley said, feigning sadness.

"Which one?"

He paused.

Careful now.

"The boy."

They were both quiet, her eyes studying his face, him studying hers. Finally, she twirled a single curl around her finger and smiled.

"Oh you poor thing. How awful! Please, can I entice you in for a tea?"

"I don't want to trouble you at all."

"Nonsense," she said, touching his arm. "Come in. We'll have a chat."

❧

SILENCE ALWAYS TROUBLED RIPLEY MORE IN LOCATIONS that were unfamiliar. At home, in restaurants and shops he frequented, at the precinct—these were all place Mark knew what to expect. He was familiar with those places before he'd lost his hearing, or at least frequented them enough with other people since the explosion. He knew what to expect, what was happening and what he might hear if he had the sense back. His brain did that a lot, filled in the blanks where silence had taken over, the memory of sound in his brain completing the story around him.

But here, in a place like this, a place he had never been, the silence was a gaping black hole, one that couldn't be filled with the memory of noises past, or even a familiar soundtrack of voices, appliances, music...

Is there a dishwasher running in the kitchen or pets barking outside? Who lives here? What is Camilla doing? Is she loading a gun or raiding the knife block?

Ripley felt vibrations in the floor and a disturbance in the air around him, though probably just from the central heating system. It was unnerving, especially given the circumstances.

A firm knock on the wall alerted him to her presence.

"I didn't want to startle you," Camilla said. "Thought I'd knock on the wall rather than barging in on you."

"That's thoughtful," Ripley said. "I've been a bit on edge as of late."

"I imagine you have been, you poor thing."

After handing him a steaming mug of coffee, she sat next to him on the couch. He looked across the coffee table at the empty sofa, willing her over there and out of his space, but she crossed her slender legs, firmly cementing herself on the cushion beside his.

"So first things first," she said, putting her hand on his knee. "Mark, what do you do?"

"I'm... a freelancer."

"Cool! Writer?"

"General work, finding out information, running errands for the city."

"Sounds intriguing."

"It's not really."

"You live in the area?"

"Apartment in town, yes."

"Apartment?" She punctuated the word with a bat of her lashes. "If I may be so bold, and I mean nothing by this, but... married?"

The answer was simple, but Ripley struggled to answer, his tongue thick and dry in his mouth.

"Oh goodness," she said, giving his knee a squeeze. "I didn't mean to—"

"Not any more," he said.

"Is she..."

"We're divorced."

Her shoulders dropped as she relaxed and exhaled.

"Thank goodness. I mean, no, divorce is awful, but at least she's not, you know…"

"Dead."

Camilla squeaked out a nervous giggle, and Ripley smiled.

"Sorry," he said. "Divorcee's sick sense of humour."

Also, she is dead.

"Tell me," she said, getting down to business. "Tell me about this family friend."

Spin this yarn good, Mark.

"They found him in a warehouse. She was… mutilated."

"Oh my," she said, her hand moving to her mouth.

"There was evidence of wooded areas, perhaps a farm, and I was wondering if you'd seen anyone odd out here, anyone who delivers to you or your neighbours."

"Why, no. I don't think so, but I haven't been watching for anything. I heard about those crimes on the news, but they were all the way in town, so…"

"There was a body found out in this direction, in a warehouse by the tracks."

She bit down on her lip, her brow furrowing.

"Oh no need to worry, it was still a good jaunt from here."

She shifted in her seat, wrapping her hands around her mug.

"So do you live here on your own, Camilla?"

Her eyes flickered to the doorway.

"I do, yes."

Lay it on thick, Ripley.

This time, he put his hand on her knee. "A beautiful woman like you? Not married?"

She pressed her plump, coral lips to the mug, taking a sip then licking her top lip.

"Sweet of you to say." Camille was beaming now. "But no. Haven't found the right prince yet."

Dear fucking Christ.

"Well, some lucky guy is missing out."

They both laughed, and she took another sip of her coffee.

"Are you nervous, out here on your own? No family to come visit?"

"I'm an only child," she said. "And my parents passed long ago. They left me this place," she said, sweeping her hand around the room. "It's more than I need, but I'm glad to have it."

"It's really a gorgeous spot," Ripley said. "Lots of land?"

"Enough," she said. "The house is certainly big enough for little ol' me, and for any... guests that might pass through." She winked. "The yard is amazing. I love to garden and hang out in the back. I have some stock in the back—few goats, quail. Just enough to keep me busy. And the eggs are delicious. Rich."

"Sounds amazing." Mark took a long, slow sip of his coffee, gearing up to take his next move.

"I'd admire you, living out here like this. I've been confined to the city with work and such. I'd love to be away from the rat race. This is like an Eden."

"Aw!" Her hand returned to Ripley's knee.

"I've never really seen an honest-to-goodness farm," he said, hoping for a tour.

"Well let's go for a stroll! Let me show you around."

"Oh I couldn't. I've already imposed—"

"Mark." She set her mug on the coffee table and put her hand on Mark's cheek. "You are too sweet. You let me worry about me. If it was an imposition, I would say. I enjoy the company. Gets pretty quiet out here."

"I bet it does," Mark said, nodding. "Hey, may I use your facilities first? I've been on the road for a bit, and the coffee..."

"Of course," she said, picking up his mug and heading to the kitchen. She nodded to the hallway. "Second door on the left."

"Thanks."

Ripley slowly made his way down the hall, looking at the photographs as he passed. Pictures of Camilla with friends, on vacation in the tropics, her graduation picture. Nothing of use.

After relieving himself and sifting through her bathroom cabinets, he came back out to the living room. Camilla was still in the kitchen, loading the dishwasher and wiping the counter. He hovered in front of the fireplace, looking at the pictures on the mantle.

Like a fist to the gut, all the wind was knocked out of him, rocking him on his feet.

"Oh."

His vision wavered between clear and pinhole as he reached for the picture, picking up the frame and holding it to his face. He blinked hard, one, two, three times, but the image remained haunting.

Camille wrapped her slender fingers around his shoulder. Her turned to face her.

"My friend, Dale," she said.

Mark felt like screaming, like throwing the picture against the wall and taking the broken shards of glass to slash at Sutherland's face.

A very young Tommy, on his knee, head tucked into Dale's chest.

"This... his boy?"

Her eye scanned the picture and grew very dark, her spritely face and energy dulling to sullen. She took the picture out of Ripley's hand and looked at it, running her finger over Sutherland's face.

"We don't speak much anymore," she said, putting the picture back on the mantle.

Her demeanor changed, with great effort it seemed. A strained smile stretched across her face and she laced her fingers through Ripley's.

"Shall we?" she said, nodding to the door.

CHAPTER 19

He sat in his car, the boy nestled in the passenger seat. He reached over and fixed the boy's cap; it was an Edmonton Oilers toque pulled down to his eyelashes, partially obscuring the absence of his eyes.

"You're better off without them."

He adjusted the boy's hoodie and wiped his face. The boy leaned towards him as he dabbed the milkshake on his lips.

He smiled. The boy was better than the others. He appreciated the effort, the change. This one had played nice.

That's the trick. The young ones. Less tainted, alone.

The boy's father had been a drunk, propping his boy outside the trailer while he screwed his trick inside. Boy wandered off all the time, down the street to the convenience store to pick up coke-bottle gummies and a pack of No. 7's to keep his daddy happy. If the boy showed up back at the trailer empty handed, he would disappear inside the trailer. The boy getting reprimanded, so loud everyone in the neighborhood could hear, the old fucker blaming the boy's behaviour on the state of society.

He wasn't wrong.

But the asshole won't be yelling at anyone again.

He looked out the window, waiting for the last customers of the day to leave so he could go pick the lot for a bit more steel. Though he put a lot of time and effort into making his tools, he didn't like to use them on more than one creation, cross contamination a constant worry. Besides, he enjoyed forging the steel, pounding it into submission, creating a tool that was just right, perfect for the delicate task at hand.

And after a number of failures, success. Finally.

And soon it would be time for another.

"We've just begun, my son."

The boy said nothing, just leaned towards him.

"Would you like to go inside?"

He tapped the door of the car and the boy's hand came up, seeking his own handle. They stepped out of the car in unison and walked towards Farm Supply.

∽

The little bell above the door chimed.

Judd was in the back room, hauling bags of barbecue charcoal out of boxes to put out on the show floor. He stood up straight, cracked his back, and hobbled out the swinging door to the front counter.

"Howdy there!" Judd hollered out before he saw his customers, happy to greet anyone to his shop.

"Hello!"

When the voice carried to him from the entrance, the hairs on the back of Judd's neck stood at attention. It was him, the man he and that Ripley fellow had talked about. Judd was sure about that. The voice was distinct, he remembered that now, crawling up his spine like a millipede.

Instead of walking straight down to greet the customer and shake his hand, Judd crept behind the counter, putting a barrier between him and the metal-seeking man.

"How are you today, good sir?" Judd asked, forcing his voice to sound chipper.

"Perfectly fine," the man said.

Judd hadn't remembered how menacing the man looked. Or he hadn't noticed. Judd told himself that it was all in his head; he thought this man looked a touch evil because all that talk with Mr. Ripley had spooked him.

This was just another man who had been friendly and courteous, never a bother.

But it wasn't just the man. For once, he wasn't alone.

A boy stood in the doorway, a wobbling waif on a wiry, frail frame, skin grey and sunken. He was badly injured, bandages over his eyes and mouth swollen.

"Hey there, young fellow," Judd said. "You look a little worse for wear. Can I interest you in a lollipop?"

The man laughed, the sound clawing the insides of Judd's guts.

"Oh, he can't hear you," the man said, smiling at the boy. "Can't speak, either. But check this out."

The man came and leaned against the counter, then stomped his heavy boot on the floor. The boy cocked his head and walked towards them until he bumped against the counter.

"Ain't that something?" the man said, glowing with glee. "Smart one, this."

It was horrible, the boys face, pale and gaunt.

"You want a lolly?"

The man took a lollypop from the bowl, unwrapped it, and put it up to the boy's lips. The boy opened his mouth and sealed his lips around stick, letting the candy sit in his mouth. He was still as a statue, other than strained swallowing.

"What's wrong with him?" Judd asked, tears in his eyes.

"Wrong? No," the man said, chortling. "Nothing wrong with him. He's better now. Deaf, blind, and dumb."

"Dumb?"

The way the stick was still, not rolling around his mouth.

"He hasn't got a tongue," the man said. The look on Judd's face was a window to the horror he felt. "Oh no, it's okay. He can still swallow. I only took the tip."

Judd stared at the man, jaw agape. The man noticed, and quickly explained. "Oh, just to prevent speech. He can still swallow."

"Ah," Judd said, trying to sound casual and unfazed.

The man stared at Judd, his eyes almost solid black. Judd smiled a laughed nervously, but the man didn't say a work. He didn't blink, didn't breath. He stared at Judd until Judd grew so uncomfortable he had to squirm away.

"All right, then, sir," Judd said, sitting down behind the counter and rearranging the cigarettes. "Let me know if you need help with anything."

"May I go back and take a look in your scrap yard?"

"Of course! I'll be right out, go right ahead. Poke around anywhere you like. Some feller dropped off an old chevy just the other day. Might have what you're lookin' for."

The man's eyes brightened and the corners of his mouth curled into a smile, revealing more of his teeth than Judd would have liked.

"That's good. Very good, indeed." The man turned to the boy and took his hand. "Better lead you, son. Lots to trip on."

The man led the boy through the aisles and out the back door to the scrap yard. Judd waited until the back door swung shut before grabbing the phone from beneath the counter. He pulled Ripley's card out of his shirt pocket and dialed.

Ring.

Ring.

Ring.

With each ring, Judd's heart pounded harder, faster, until the call went to voicemail.

"Mr. Ripley, it's Judd. From the farm supply. Could you please give me a call as soon as you can? Or, ya know, if it's not bother... it's just... can you pop by? Now? He's here, and it's really weird, but there's this boy—"

A loud crash from outside started Judd, and he dropped the phone. He sat still for a moment, listening for other noises, then put the phone back on the receiver. As he passed through the aisles on the way to the back door, he grabbed a crowbar and held it against his leg.

It was bright outside, the last throes of daylight fires burning low in the sky. Judd shielded his eyes as he walked between the rows of mower and junk cars, looking for his customers.

"You folks doing all right, then?"

Nothing but birds twittering in the trees and the occasional whoosh of traffic on the road. Judd took slow, calculated steps, acutely aware of the noise of the gravel crunching beneath his boots. He spotted the hood of the Chevy in the back corner. It was ajar, a menacing wave.

Judd approached cautiously, peering in at the engine. The components under the hood had been picked apart, by either this man or others. A wrench and metal cutters had been placed on the engine, and an oily cloth tossed on the ground beside the vehicle. Judd straightened up and looked around to see if the man was nearby. He wasn't, but the boy was, standing by the box of the truck. Judd went over to him, looking around for the man, who was no where to be seen. Judd stood in front of the boy and gently placed his hands on his shoulders.

"Son," Judd whispered.

The boy responded to Judd's breath on his face, his face twitching ever so slightly. Judd stroked his cheek, and the boy leaned into the gentle touch.

"What had happened to you, young man?"

The man forgotten about, the murders and Ripley and the vet clinic not even a glimmer of a thought in his mind, Judd wrapped his arms around the boy and embraced him in a hug. At first the boy was stiff as a board, resisting the attention, but Judd persisted, holding him close and talking to him.

"It's okay. Whatever's gone on, it's okay. I've got you now."

The boy melted into Judd's embrace, resting his arm against the man's chest and going limp in his arms. Shuddering sobs escaped from the boy's mouth in wet burst, the sound garbled over his mutilated tongue. He grabbed onto Judd's arms, driving his fingers into Judd's biceps and clinging for dear life.

Judd would have held on forever, held on until Mr. Ripley arrived and put that horrible man in cuffs. He would have held on until that boy was safe and happy and healthy.

But he couldn't.

A jolt shattered the love, spearing through his back and punching through his stomach. The boy jumped back, surprised, as a shard of steel poked him in the belly. Judd's hand's found the protrusion sticking out his gut just below the middle of his ribcage, chunks of meat and bone pushed out down his favourite plaid shirt.

"Oh shucks," Judd said, blood sputtering out with his words.

The man circled around and stood beside the boy. He had a smug look smeared across his face.

"Meddling old fool," the man said. "First of all, mind your own business. Sell your shit and keep your assumptions to yourself."

Judd fell to his knees, grasping at the rebar sticking

through his body. He couldn't take his eyes off the boy's face, his pale, youthful skin…

"Second, who did you call? Where has your meddling taken you, and what does it mean for me?"

Fear. Sadness. Terror and pain. The boy's face alluded to nothing before, but now it was a plethora of emotion, contorted, quivering, his mouth forming words and voice rising in his belly.

"Oooh," the boy moaned. His hands reached out, seeking Judd. "Elb! Elb!"

The boy was convulsing, panicked. He stumbled forward, finding Judd with the tips of his sneakers. The boy dropped to his needs, his hands reaching Judd, crawling up his legs until he found the old man's belly and the offending piece of rebar. His hands groped around the metal, his fingers slipping through the blood and exploring the damaged tissue.

"O mo mo," the boy garbled.

A hard and quavering sigh came from deep within the boy's belly. He sniffled, his lip trembling violently.

He knows.

"It's okay, young buck," Judd said, taking a hand off his belly and ruffling the boy's hair. "I was close to expiring anyways. Gettin' a bit sour, so they say."

Judd looked up at the man, his satisfied smile poisoning his wretched, pretty face.

"And you," he said, tapping the boy's chest. "You will be just fine. I got this."

"Enough, old man," the man said, kneeling down beside Judd and the boy. "And one last item for your consideration..."

The man grabbed the rebar and wrenched it back and forth, hauling it up higher through Judd's body, open a geyser of blood and tearing through organs. The boy screamed as he was elbowed to the side by the man. Judd howled in agony but did not fight back, allowing the man to take his tantrum out on him rather than the boy.

"Never, ever, ever interfere with my creation," the man said, motioning to the boy.

Judd knew. Looking at the boy, hearing those awful words...

His creation.

"Mister," Judd said, his voice quiet and wet.

His next words were silent. Intentionally.

The man leaned forward, trying to hear what Judd was saying.

With every bit of strength Judd had left, he launched forward, sinking his teeth into the man's cheek. The man howled as Judd clamped down, pulling and gnawing until he tore a sizable chunk of flesh from the man's cheek. The man stood and stumbled back, hand over his fresh wound, a look of shock and horror on his disfigured face. Judd smiled, sting clamped between his teeth, blood dribbling down his chin.

Then he slumped over in a pile on the ground, that smile frozen on his face as he breathed his last breath.

"FUCK!"

He held his face, gagging at the blood running through his fingers.

The old man slumped to the ground, eyes open, chest still.

"Goddamit!" the man yelled, kicking a spray of gravel at Judd.

Pelted by collateral gravel, the boy's crying escalated and a wet spot spread on the front of his jeans.

"Oh for fuck sake."

The old man's hollering...

The phone call...

This little brat's mewling...

Sigh.

"Okay."

There was a mess of blood everywhere. The boy's hand's were drenched in crimson, his face nearing the old man's bloody handprint. The ground was a pool of blood, and he, himself, was drenched in the stuff, his face spurting and dribbling onto his new linen button-up.

"Fucking Christ!" he screamed, kicking more gravel.

Think think think

No time to clean up

Someone heard this bloody racket

And that phone call...

"Time to go," he said, grabbing the boy by the arm and yanking him towards the side of the building.

It's fine. It's fine. It's fine. I'm gloved, the kid, well, they might identify him, but they'll never find me.

When they reached the car, he tossed the kid in the backseat and laid him down, covering him up with a blanket. In a flash he slid behind the wheel, fired out the engine, and was pulling out of the parking lot, leaving a trail of dust and death behind. As he took a right on the highway, a car approached from the left.

It's okay. It's nothing. It's nothing.

It was something. The car slowed, and its blinker lit like a beacon, flashing deep into his brain.

He cranked the steering wheel and hit the gas, fish-tailing out onto the highway, pelting gravel in his wake.

JUDD BLINKED.

And it felt glorious.

He had held a vacant stare as long as he could, feigning death while that animal cussed and fussed.

He stilled his breath and listened. He listened to the car engine fire up, and the crunch of tires on gravel. Then a violent rev and rustle in the gravel and a screech down the highway. And then... something else.

More crunching.

Another car coming in the parking lot.

Judd smiled.

After sucking in a painful breath, Judd buried his fingers in his belly knuckle deep, then reached out to a nearby sheet of tin, his fingers dancing manically over the metal. Another dip into his wound, another scribble. He kept scrawling and dipping until the setting sun darkened, fading from pink, to grey, to nothing...

CHAPTER 20

"I like to sit out here and read sometimes, or just sit and sip tea while I listen to nature."

Camilla sat on the Adirondack chair on the lawn, looking lovingly at the woods.

Mark thought it really was quite beautiful. Secluded, a good chunk of land buried in the woods. If it wasn't for his morbid suspicions, it would be a veritable Eden.

"That boy," Mark said.

"Yes."

He didn't have to ask the question. The look on her face told Mark she knew exactly what he was wondering. He had no idea what to expect. No idea what the hell was going on.

"My son."

What?

Butterflies flapped around inside Mark's stomach, a sense of elation, confusion, hesitant elation.

"*Your* son?"

Quiet rested between them for a moment while she pressed the edge of her lip on her glass of iced tea. Mark thought of Tommy of the surveillance video, of his mind falling prey to stress and the power of suggestion.

It wasn't Tommy at all. It was this boy.

"My son." She swallowed hard.

Mark reached over and took her hand. She looked up at him, tears in her eyes.

Oh no.

If he's dead, then...

"Camilla, is he... gone?"

A tear escaped, rolling down her rosy cheek and slipping onto her leg. "I haven't seen him ages."

Mark's mind was noisy, a thousand questions rattling around. He let them percolate, trying to be gentle, trying to find the right ones.

"How old is he, Camilla?"

"Twenty-four."

Tommy's age.

Tommy's hair colour, from the look at that photograph.

"Do you... when did you last see him?"

She swiped away another trail of tears and waved her

hand at Mark. "Look at me, all foolish, and we've only just met."

Shit. Shut down.

He patted her hand, signaling he would drop it.

"What about you? Any children?"

"One. Tommy. About the same age as your boy."

"Oh lovely! And you keep in touch?"

"Oh yes. It was a struggle for us, after the accident, but we are still close. Getting closer, in fact."

"That's good," she said, the smile returning to her lips.

Holy shit. There it is. A chance.

"Do you want to see a photograph?"

"I sure do!"

Mark pulled his phone from his pocket, scrolled through his pictures, and pulled up a recent shot of Tommy at the bar.

"Good boy, my Tommy. Runs his own business. He's turned into a really great guy."

Camilla took the phone from Mark's hand and studied the picture. Her face changed, her mouth tightening to a tight line and a crease wrinkling between her eyes.

"This is your son?" she asked.

"Um... yeah."

She handed the phone back and gulped the remainder of her iced tea.

"Looks like a lovely young man," she said, not a hint of a smile on her face.

Mark finished his iced tea, and she stood from her chair. "Would you like to see the rest of the property?"

"Sure, yes."

They walked along the back fence, Camilla telling him the name of each goat that came up to nibble them. She spoke of the history of the area, the care facility nearby, the little town of Picton a half hour away. She had been there her whole life, she said, but made no mention of a spouse or boyfriend to coincide with that son. Didn't mention the kid at all, in fact.

When they got to the front of the barn, she rolled open the door, and a plume of dust coughed out into the late-day sun.

"Sorry," she said, waving a hand in front of her face. "Don't come in here as often as I should."

The garage was half full of lawn equipment, a rusted out old orange mustang with a blue door, and various and assorted tools. Everything was covered in a fine coating of dust and seemingly held together by an intricate weave of spiders webs. When they stepped inside, a trio of rats skittered across the floor and through a hole in the back wall.

"Used to park my car in here, but it's a real hassle to haul that door up and down. Not electric, you see, and

I've been too cheap to have someone come put power to it. For the amount I use it, it's unnecessary."

"Is there a side door you can come in and out to get the yard stuff?"

She hesitated.

He watched her, then had a quick glance around the interior of the barn.

There's something here.

"No, no need. I have someone come take care of my yard maintenance. He brings all his equipment with him."

"Yard maintenance?"

Mark was almost giddy. He stepped out of the barn and looked around at the bar, feigning interest.

"Your yard is beautiful? Who does your maintenance?

Is it this son? The bloke from the farm supply store?

Camilla didn't have a chance to answer. Mark phone rang, breaking the roll. He ignored it.

"Shouldn't you get that?"

"Naw, it's okay. I'm not a very important guy. Probably just telemarketers."

Mark pulled the phone from his pocket, not wanting to appear too desperate in his questioning about the lawn guy. He looked at the number, but didn't recognize it. It stopped ringing, and he slid it back in his pocket.

"If it's important, they'll leave a message."

"It's been so lovely having a visitor," Camilla said, clearly trying to urge him to leave.

"You've been a gracious host," Mark said, kissing her hand. "Maybe we could—"

His phone pinged.

Voicemail.

An unsettled niggle crawled up Mark's spine.

"Yes, it was a pleasure meeting you, Camilla," he said, as he pulled his keys from his pocket.

"Oh I hope I was of some help."

"You certainly were," he lied, knowing he was leaving with more questions than he came. "And a pleasant respite from my personal hurricane."

She smiled and kissed him on the cheek.

As soon as Mark was on the highway, he brought up the transcript of the voicemail on his phone.

"Mr. Ripley? It's Judd from the farm supply…"

Poor old fella could be just rattled. Mark riled him up earlier with talk of the crimes, and of this man. But Judd was genuinely freaked out. Overactive imagination or not, Mark needed to check it out.

He pinned it towards the shop. It was a clear cut line from the farm on Faulten Drive, and traffic was thin, so Mark was able to get there in just twenty minutes, just at the edge of dusk. He slowed the Fairlane, approaching the opening of the parking lot as a maroon Crown Victoria pulled up to the road from the parking lot of the farm supply store. It paused for a moment, then spun its tires and fishtailed out onto the highway, leaving rubber behind as it screeched off in the opposite direction. Mark turned into the lot, burning the memory of the car into his brain.

The little bell rang, announcing his arrival. Judd, however, did not greet him.

"Judd! It's Mark Ripley!"

No answer.

Mark had a quick look around the store, hitting the aisles at nearly a sprint, then burst out the back door.

"Judd!"

He scoured the lawn equipment as he passed, but went straight for the old cars. There were a few sedans and a station wagon, but the old Ford truck with its hood up caught his eye. He didn't reach the car before seeing Judd on the ground."

"Ah shit."

It was too late, but just. Judd had no pulse, but he was warm, the blood soaking into the ground beneath him still wet. A piece of rebar was speared straight through him, back to front, and he was covered in blood. His clothes, his face...

Upon closer inspection, there were handprints on his

shirt. Smaller handprints. And on his face, one on each cheek.

Not the killer.

Whoever this hand print belonged to was holding Judd's face. Tenderly.

Judd's hands were covered in blood, but on his right, the fingers were coated to the knuckle, except for the pad of his pointer finger, which was white. Didn't take long to discover the piece of naked tin with Judd's artwork marring the surface.

It was a crude drawing of a face, x's for eyes, x's for ears, and an x over the mouth.

Mark called an ambulance, then phoned the police station directly and gave them the address. After emergency services had been activated, Mark called Sutherland, but got no answer. He called the police station directly.

"No sorry, Mr. Ripley," Maggie, the receptionist said. "Left long ago, of course."

"How long?"

"Well, never came back from lunch. Said he had some personal business to attend to."

"Mmmm."

Mark shut down his phone and looked over the scene, staring into the face of the bloody happy face.

CHAPTER 21

The boy was clean. As soon as they arrived home, he had whisked him to the bathroom and striped him down to his boxers and meticulously cleaned every drop of blood from his skin, including that which was stuck beneath his nails. He even made the boy brush his teeth, in case any nastiness got in his mouth.

Once he was certain that the boy was clean, he led him to his room and gave him a fresh change of clothes, including boxers. He left the boy to dress on his own, respectful of his privacy. Besides, he needed to shower the filth off himself, and despite the fact he'd removed the boy's eyes from the equation, he wanted his privacy, too.

Blood swirled in tendrils down the drain as he scrubbed himself from head to toe. With a nail brush he scrubbed until the tips off his fingers were raw, and then he scrubbed some more. He stepped out of the shower and patted himself off with a towel before heading to his lab.

He unrolled his leather satchel on the counter and ran his finger over the array of instruments he'd created, each a little different, each waiting for their own part of his creation. He'd gone through a fair few with the last patient, one of which he'd left behind at the hospital after having to remove his speech on the fly.

"I'll need a few new ones for my next one."

He considered the tools, taking a mental inventory of his needs, then rolled them up and tucked the satchel back in a drawer.

"Further to that," he said, rubbing his hands together, "I'll need a next one."

On the wall behind the dental chair was a collage of photographs and notes, pictures of each of his creations. The first were crude, homeless men he neglected to clean properly, undiagnosed conditions that impeded their healing. After a few of those he graduated to young men stumbling home drunk from the bar or running in the park. Though his drugs were strong, this type of subject was tricky, with a high potential of outpouring him while he was doing his work.

The latest three: the man from the vet clinic, the confetti man in the box, and the boy. He had taken the boy first, months before the other two, and while he was healing, he took the young security guard from the vet clinic. Poor sap was just keeping the place while his parents were vacationing in Florida. But a need for a sedative had arisen, and the closed clinic was convenient, as was he, the next victim.

"But you didn't work out, did you," he said, stoking the photograph with his finger. "Squirmed too much. The ears are a delicate task, my friend, those itty bitty little bones and ducts. The slightest nick and there's big trouble in little canal."

A giggle started in his belly, forming into manic laughter that echoed through the lab. After a minute, he composed himself and caught his breath.

"Oooh, wasn't I mad," he said. "Jammed that fucking bone straight through your damn head. And next!"

He dragged his finger across the board to the confetti man.

"And you. You were almost a success. It was to be a public unveiling. Your birthday! Even confetti for them when they found you and unwrapped you." His smile turned to a scowl. "But I didn't think that through, either. You weren't tamed before I let you out into the wild."

He waggled his tongue out, poking it with his finger. "Silence requires two organs, not just one. You couldn't hear the hateful rhetoric around you, but you could spew it. Then other's would hear."

A picture of the boy, a photograph he snapped after following him from school one day. "You. Though I had to go back and take your tongue after everything else was already healed, the rest was a glittering success story, if I do say so myself."

He bowed to the wall and let out a royal wave to his imaginary audience.

"And now, ladies and gentlemen. Round two shall commence shortly."

CHAPTER 22

The precinct was a ghost town, just a few rookies rolling through like tumbleweeds, jittery and hopped up on coffee, and Maggie manning the front desk.

"Howdy, Mark!" she said. Her sing-song tones never did match the situation, Mark thought, though it was a pleasant ray of sunshine in a world of storms of blood and death. "How goes it?"

"Sutherland back yet?" he asked as he passed behind the counter, heading to his makeshift office.

"Never came back. Don't expect him to, at this hour."

It was full dark outside, the night shift clattering about back in the locker room. Evidence would be coming in soon from the farm supply, and Mark wanted to stay on top of it. There were some good samples from the small prints, the old Ford, and the surrounding crime scene. It was very sloppy, this time. Unplanned.

"The old man was on to you."

Mark ruffled his fingers through his hair, tears welling in his eyes.

"Goddamnit."

The pictures stared back at him, eyeless corpses, heads mutilated.

Mark printed out the pic on his phone—the blood-drawn happy face with the X's—and pinned it to the board beside the shots of the victims.

"Okay, Judd. What are you saying?"

Mark paced back and forth, talking to the face.

"No eyes, no ears, no tongue. See no evil, hear no evil, speak no evil."

He flipped through the files, pulling up the quick sheet on each of the victims.

"Who are you guys? Snitches? Why is he silencing you?"

The first a young man, early twenties, tongue intact. The second, a middle-aged man, tongue initially intact.

"Until you began to talk, you old fucker."

Sarah. The old lady in Sarah's place. Both sloppy, impulsive.

"Not part of the plan. Connected, but not to his purpose."

Sarah.

"To me?"

His mind wandered to Tommy, and the speed of his pacing increased, threading to wear a trench in the carpet.

Who is this woman on the farm?

And this kid, the one that looks like my Tommy? That's too much of a coincidence.

"Sutherland."

Dale had some explaining to do. Was this his kid? And why had Mark never heard about this woman who was all over Dale in those photographs? And that child, on his knee.

Mark left the conference room and went to Sutherland's office, first checking that no one was around or paying attention. They were buddies, so people shouldn't think much of it, but you never know who might decide to snoop and gossip. And, one of the disadvantages of not having hearing is that you can't hear people coming.

Sutherland's office was unlocked, which made it a breeze to slip and close the door. The blinds were already drawn, so Mark was able to dive right in. He flipped through the papers on the desk, finding nothing other than department paperwork, junk mail, and company memos. The drawers contained nothing useful, either, just stationary supplies, a small bottle of Jameson, and a skin magazine. There were no pictures on his desk, and the framed art on his walls looked like it came from Ikea.

Mark sat in the chair and riffled through the papers on the desk, having a closer look. He got the paperwork on the lab results from the notes, and had a closer look.

Though the samples were small, they were big enough to make a match. Tommy was in the system for a drug-related arrest a few years before, so his name popped up. The gender was male so it couldn't be Sarah...

A buzzing. A slight niggle in his brain kept chirping at him, telling him to go deeper.

He picked up Sutherland's phone.

"Jackie? Are you around?" Mind if I come down? I need you to help me clear something up."

BY THE TIME MARK GOT DOWN TO THE LAB IN THE basement, Jackie Fields already had the evidence pulled, and was scrolling through data on the computer.

"Mark." She stood when he came in the room, going to him and embracing him in a hug. She didn't let go, and he didn't pull away. She felt good, safe. This was not the time to visit this feeling, but one day.

"What are you looking for," she said, pulling away and returning to the computer. Though she sat in front of the screen, her full attention was on Mark.

"The specimen samples," Mark said. "The notes."

"Uh huh."

Judging by the flush in her cheeks, she knew which results he wanted to discuss.

"It's okay," he said. "I know. Tommy."

She nodded. "Perhaps."

"Perhaps?"

A deer in headlights, she struggled to explain. "I thought... I assumed Dale would have told you."

Cool and collected, Mark. Don't let her think there's trouble.

"Yeah," he said. "We've talked about so much. It's been a really hard time, especially with Sarah. And Tommy."

"Of course," Jackie said. The side-eye told him, clearly, she didn't buy it.

"Well, the blood sample was small, just the scratches on the notes, but we were able to lift partial specimens. We got a three-quarters match. Tommy's name came up when we plugged it in the system, but it's not necessarily his blood."

"What? How so?"

"Well there are commonalities, but not a hundred percent. This could be a margin of error, or not the right person."

"Anyone else is the system?"

"We only ran the criminal system," she said. "Want me to run in in all the servers? Criminal records checks and such?"

"If you wouldn't mind."

"Might take a bit. The systems are deep."

"No problem," Mark said. "Thanks for doing this."

"Hey," she said, flashing that gorgeous, ruby smile at him. "Anything. Any time. Seriously."

Mark smiled, a genuine happiness, and punctuated it with a yawn.

"Here's an idea," she said, standing from her chair and putting her hands on his shoulder. "Why don't you go home. Get some sleep."

"Sleep is for the weak," he laughed.

Wrapping her arms around him once again, she punctuated the embrace by brushing her lips against his before returning to her computer screen.

MARK KNEW FIELDS WAS RIGHT. HE SHOULD GO HOME, have a bite to eat, catch some shut eye. But he needed to make one more stop, just to sate his hunger for the truth. At least give it a little snack.

He pulled the Fairlane a block back from Sutherland's apartment complex, behind Wally's convenience store in a spot behind the dumpster. It wasn't a fool-proof hiding spot, but definitely harder to spot than parking in front of the building. He needed the fresh air, anyways, to clear his head. He could lose himself on a walk, the sounds of the city mere vibrations beneath his skin, the rushing traffic just disturbances in the air.

It felt like the explosion all over again. His life was unraveling, piece by piece, and he was just pulling at the threads and making it worse. Tommy, Sarah, Sutherland. Even poor old Judd. There were more questions than answers, and the information was garbled in Mark's head. For not being able to hear, he was often frustrated at how loud it was in his head.

A few minutes and Mark was at the top of the steps, walking in the first door, wondering what he was going to say. Would Sutherland even let him in? They had fought last time they'd seen each other, but that was their MO.

You're over thinking this, Ripley.

A young couple passed through the secure door, giggling and fully engrossed in each other, providing the perfect opportunity to get in the building unannounced. Mark took the elevator to the fourth floor, his anxiety rising with each floor. When he stepped off the elevator, his heart was threatening to pound straight out his ears.

Why am I so nervous? What do I expect to find?

No use delaying it, Mark banged on the door. While he waited for a response, he ran over dialogue in his head, planning what her would say to Dale and how he would say it. After a minute, he banged on the door again, then waited for signs of life. When it was clear no one was home, or he wasn't going to answer, Mark decided bold measures were necessary. He took his pick out of his pocket, breaking his way into his friends apartment.

If he'd been home, Mark had fully prepared to tell him that he had been worried, and he was checking on him. But thankfully, the apartment was pitch black. Mark did a quick sweep, ensuring that Sutherland was not home before going on a deeper search.

But what am I looking for?

Sutherland's mail was stacked on the counter, bills, bank statements, junk mail. His calendar was pretty empty, a few dates written in on Friday nights and an appointment for an oil change. Mark went to the living room, checking over the shelves filled with DVD's and picture frames. There were pictures of Dale during the force golf tournaments, a few snaps of Dale and some ex-girlfriends, a picture and him and Mark in uniform.

Mark picked up the picture, staring at the younger version of him, scar free, not a care in the world. Life was good, then, when people didn't look at him like he was broken, and hesitate to communicate with him because of his disability. He'd give anything to go back, to not go in that warehouse, to still have his hearing, his job, his life.

But that's that, I suppose.

Mark set the picture down and keep looking through Sutherland's stuff, snooping through drawers and move junk around tables. The bedroom was pretty bare—a double bed, a three drawer dresser, and a small night-stand. The bedside table had a bluetooth speaker on it, and headphones in the drawer. The dresser was full of clothes, crudely folded and bunched up, but little else.

Great.

Nothing. Even though Mark had no idea what he was looking for, he was upset he hadn't found it. He shuffled back out into the living room, giving the room one last look. A stack of books below the coffee table caught his attention. He sat on the couch and pulled out the stack. A couple car magazines, a tool catalogue, a coffee table book about UFO's, and a photo album.

Bingo.

It was a fat album, stuffed with a variety of pictures from Sutherland's school years, a handful of family photos, including his parents, aunts, uncles, and cousins, and shot of friends and others Mark had never met. Some were from Dale's younger years, before Mark knew him, and some were from his adult years.

And there she was, Camilla, Dale's arm around her and the little boy on his knee. Same photo Camilla had in her house. It was the only photo of them—the only photo of Camilla or the kid, in fact—and it had been folded, tucked behind another photo on the page. Flipping forward, Mark found more of the Dale he knew, company picnics, hanging out with him, Sarah, and Tommy.

Mark kept the photo. He'd have to come clean and

talk to Sutherland about all of this, anyways. Better to have the picture in case Sutherland played dumb.

After putting the books back the way they were, Mark quietly left the apartment and followed the shadows back to his car. Once he was behind the wheel, he realized how exhausted he really was. He aimed the Fairlane for home, hoping a good night's rest might clear the fog.

CHAPTER 23

The bar was in full swing, shoulder-to-shoulder people dancing, drinking, the band blaring out hair band tunes. Sutherland shouldered his way through the crowd, peering over the bar at Randall who was too slammed to notice him come in. He scanned the crowd for Tommy, but didn't see him, which wasn't surprising considering the mass of people moving around and gyrating like worms.

After making the rounds two or three times, and checking the bathrooms compete with stalls, Sutherland decided to bite the bullet and converse with the brute. Sutherland walked up to the bar, leaning on the sticky wood and giving it a few harp raps with his knuckles. Randall turned to the sound, but stood still, not quite sure what to do.

"A drink?" Sutherland said.

Randall nodded. He kept an eye on Sutherland while he pulled a bourbon from under the cupboard. After sliding the drink along the bar, Randall maintained eye contact while Sutherland raised the glass in a cheers before downing it in two gulp. He set the glass down on the counter, hard, and stared at Randall.

"Another?" Randall said.

Sutherland nodded. He downed the second drink as quick as the first. Randall was about to pour another, but Sutherland held up his finger and said one word.

"Tommy."

Sutherland stared hard, his eyes never leaving Randall's face. Randall shifted from foot to foot, trying to avoid Sutherland's demanding gaze.

"Not here. Out getting supplies."

"Supplies," Sutherland repeated.

It was subtle, a minuscule flick, but it was there. Randall couldn't help but look at the back door leading to Tommy's apartment.

Sutherland smiled. "Another," he said, tapping the counter.

Randall poured up a third bourbon, which Sutherland devoured before laughing.

"Randall." Sutherland slid the glass across the counter. "You're a good man, and loyal to your boss. But you just aren't that bright."

Randall face scrunched in distaste as Sutherland peeled his arms off the sticky bar and headed to Tommy's apartment.

"TOMMY!"

The door was unlocked, but all the lights were off. Sutherland walked right in, flicking on the light slide he owned the place.

"Tommy, are you here?"

No signs of life. By the smell of it, Tommy'd been having a rough time. There was a pizza box on the coffee table, grease soaked straight through the cardboard. A liquor glass sat on the coffee table, an empty whiskey bottle beside.

"Hell of a time, looks like."

The party continued to the bathroom, where a razor and skiff of white power was laid on a mirror shard from the shattered mirror over the sink.

"Jesus kid."

His hand still in leather gloves, Sutherland swept the glass, razor, and all into the trashcan and carried it out to the kitchen where he emptied it into the kitchen garbage. Only took about five minutes, but he cleaned up the rest of the garbage and dishes before checking out the bedroom.

"What the hell do you want? Did he send you here to arrest me?"

Tommy was on the bed, laying on his back, wearing nothing more than a worn-out pair of briefs. His skin was a sallow grey, his fingers raw and bloody. Sutherland walked over and touched his hand.

"What the hell happened to you?"

Tommy sat up, and Sutherland grimaced.

"Bar fight. Came home feeling shitty the other night, sparred with an asshole that needed to be bounced anyways."

Sutherland touched the side of Tommy's face, battered and bloody.

"You're a fucking mess."

"You want something?"

Sutherland sighed and sat down on the bed next to Tommy.

"How deep under are you?"

"Halfway to China."

"Drink?"

"8 ball, too."

Sutherland looked into Tommy's eyes, tired, sunken orbs, crackled red and watery. Tommy's head seemed heavy, wobbling on his shoulders, threatening to drop off to the floor like a bowling ball.

"Okay, kiddo. You're gonna have to get yourself together."

"And why is that?" Tommy said, hauling himself to his feet. "I don't have to listen to you. Am I under arrest?"

"I would never do that to you, Tommy."

"Bullshit! You want to pin those crimes on me, the ones that are fucking him up so much."

"Look, Ripley got himself into his own slump—"

"No," Tommy said. "He didn't."

Sutherland stood and grasped Tommy's shoulders. "Boy. It's time."

Tommy said nothing.

"You hear what I'm saying?"

Tommy nodded, his lip quivering.

"We're gonna have to tell him."

CHAPTER 24

Sarah took Mark's hand, holding it in her lap.

"I love you, you know."

The sound of her voice was sweet as soft, just as he remembered.

Long tendrils of auburn hair cascaded over her shoulders, wisps of it clinging to the yellow sundress. That was his favourite dress.

"Shall we have lunch outside today?"

The sun was high but soft, a gentle heat tingling the hairs on his arm. He looked over the yard, emerald green grass shimmering in the wind, the sprays of wildflower a bright palate of rainbows.

This is not my yard, he thought.

But it didn't matter. Because Sarah was there, the day

was beautiful, and he could hear the birds singing their poems through the trees.

They walked, arm in arm, to the Adirondack chairs in the middle of the yard. Before sitting, Sarah pressed her lips against his, mouth moist, her breath warm.

"I love you," she breathed into his mouth.

They sat, so many hours they sat, the sun rising and setting then rising again, never tiring of each other's company, of the beauty of the world, of the chitter and chatter of the fauna in the yard. Goats stroll by, nibbling at their fingertips, looking for a handout. Mark laughed as one licked his palm, its tongue rough and teasing.

"Sarah, I am so, so happy."

When he looked up at his wife, she was smiling, wide, mouth open, contorted into a broken grin.

"Happy," she repeated, but the word wasn't quite right. It was distorted, ruined by her now-tongueless maw. Goats were up standing on her legs, biting at her face, one pulling out an eyeball that stretched from her head, still attached to its tendons. Blood poured from her ears and the goats penetrated them with sharp tongues, licking out tiny bones and seeing them on the front of her dress.

"No," Mark said, frozen, unable to save her. "Not the dress."

Two goats ran off, each with an eyeball squelched between their teeth. Sarah was still smiling, her eye sockets empty, bloodied caverns, her yellow dress now solid crimson, fully soaked in blood. Her mouth puckered as her lips tightened together, a great effort to form a single word.

"Silence."

Like a vacuum, all sound was sucked from the air.

Mark screamed. He knew he was screaming, he throat strained and throbbed, but he couldn't even feel it. He felt nothing, The air had gone dead, and the colour started to drain from the world around him as if someone had pulled a plug, the glorious greens and yellows and red sailing down into the ground until the world was a blanket of grey, dead and still and silent...

Vibration.

Soft.

Growing stronger...

Mark awoke with a start, his phone trying repeatedly to get his attention. He fumbled for it, finally managing to get ahold of it and open his text messages. There was a string of texts from Jackie Fields.

Mark.

Are you okay?

Don't want to bother you, but I have a hit on those specimens.

I need to talk to you, Mark.

Mark poked at the screen, texting back.

Sorry.

I was sleeping. Bad dream.

Want me to come down there?

Mark looked at his clock. Holy shit! 6pm? I slept all goddamn day!

I'm on my way to you now, Mark.

Mark sat straight up in bed. Jackie was coming to his place. She had never come to his place.

It was something important. And it couldn't wait.

THE HEADLIGHTS OF MARK'S FAIRLANE CUT THROUGH THE night, lighting the softly fallen snow like shooting stars on the highway. He was going fast, too fast for comfort, but he was in a hurry to get there. Enough was enough. No beating around the bush anymore, no sleepless night and panic attacks. Time to attack this head on.

Jackie fields was beside him, her hand on his leg as he drove, saying something to him he could not see. Visibility was shit, and his speed high, so he didn't dare turn to look at her face.

The mouth of the drive appeared in the headlights, a hungry maw ready to swallow them whole. Mark cranked the wheel at a tilt, ripping the car onto gravel drive and spraying gravel as he entered the tunnel of trees. When he emerged onto the property on the other side, he hit the brakes.

Jackie was speaking, loud enough he could hear the vibrations, but still, he didn't turn. His eyes were fixes on the driveway beside the house, and the two cars parked in tandem.

Sutherland's police cruiser, and a burgundy Crown Victoria.

"Motherfuckers."

Despite Jackie tugging on his arm, pleading with him, he parked the car, jumped out, and charged towards the door. It was so, so loud, the possibilities screaming in his head, the noise of his pounding heart threatening to drive him mad. As he grasped the door handle, the world went silent, the only noise a single voice in his head.

Mark. Stop.

Sarah's voice was calm and sweet, but sad.

"Sorry, Sarah."

Mark turned the handle and barged inside.

They were there, in the kitchen, Sutherland sitting at the table, Camilla standing by the counter.

"YOU BLOODY FOOL!" CAMILLA SHOUTED, STABBING A finger through the air at Sutherland. He was seated at the table, head in his hands. "I'm tired of this, tired of you and the reminders of what you are constantly being thrown in my face."

"I know he said," clear defeat in his tone.

"You abandoned me, Dale. "All these years."

"Look," he said, "I did what I could, gave you money—"

"It wasn't enough! It's not enough! We could have been a family, Dale."

"No!" He slammed his fists down on the table. "We were never going to be a family, Camilla. Ever. You've got a screw loose. What I should have done is never let you around that child—"

The plate smashed on the wall, narrowly missing Sutherland's head.

"I did what was right," she growled. "The world is a terrible place, Dale. Horrible. The hate, the racism, the sexual violence." She glared at him, tears of hot rage in her eyes. "He's the end of all that, don't you see?"

"You're fucking nuts."

As Sutherland reached into his pocket to pull out his phone, Mark came crashing through the door. Marks face was soaked with tears, and his fists were clenched.

Oh shit. Here we go.

"Mark, I can explain, Sutherland said, setting down his phone and holding up his hands.

"Quiet!" Mark shouted, pointing at Sutherland. "I'll hear from you in a minute."

"Oh Mr. Ripley," Camilla said, walking to him and reaching for his arm.

"No," he said, his voice gentler than when he had addressed Sutherland. "Camilla, I'm sorry you're caught in the middle of this. I know you weren't forthcoming with me the other day, but no hard feelings. This is about him and I."

Mark turned to Sutherland. "Where's Tommy?"

"We need to talk about this—"

"WHERE'S TOMMY?"

Sutherland stood still, lips sealed tight. He shifted from foot to foot before sitting back down at the table.

"You know what, Mark? No. You and I are gonna hash this out before we bring the boy into this."

No sooner had Sutherland gave the command, Mark struck him in the temple with the butt of his gun. Sutherland teetered in the chair, leaning forward, and Mark struck him again, landing the blow on the back of his head. With a crash, Sutherland collapsed to the floor.

"Okay," Mark said, turning to Camilla. "Where's my Tommy?"

That sweet, flirtation face was no longer. In its place was a sly, venomous bitch.

"Wouldn't you like to fucking know."

Mark smiled. He did know. She'd given away the tell,

the one all cops look for when asking questions. For a moment, though brief, her eyes had flickered outside to the barn.

'Thanks," Mark said, charging through the back door.

The barn was dark, but a security light blinked on when he ran up the side of the building. Like Camilla had the day before, he rolled up the barn door. It was just how they had left it, with nothing out of place, and no Tommy. Mark walked along the wall, running his hands over the plastic-covered insulation, the tools, the wood. He paused at the back wall, looking from roof to floor, wall to wall.

There's something.

Camilla had been odd when he'd asked about a back door.

Mark eyed the barn, the walls...

"Mark." Jackie came in the barn just as Mark was walking out. "What's going on?"

Mark didn't answer. He charged past her and up the side of the building, talking to himself and sizing up the wall. When he got to the back wall of the barn, he ran his hand along the wood, pushing on the boards, looking for anything out of place. After curving around to the other side, his fingers found a loose board. He pulled it out, exposing a handle. A heave and a pull, and the large red door swung open.

It was dark and dank inside. Mark's feet padded across the tight loam floor, his fingers following along the wall. The room was narrow, three meters wide and the length of the back wall of the barn. Mark walked along the hall, tapping the dirt with a toe until he was answered with a knock. As he was about to plunge his fingers into the dirt to lift the hatch door, it flew open on its own, knocking Mark back on his ass.

Light flooded the room, beaming from the basement below. A figure stumbled up the stairs, panting and frantic, and stumbled over Mark, landing face first in the dirt. Both men stopped, shocked.

"Dad?"

Flickering lights, flashing, pulsing. Everything came into focus very slowly, the nipple light on the kitchen ceiling, Camilla's angry face.

"Really fucked this one up, didn't you?"

She was smiling, quite pleased with how everything was going down.

"You wretched bitch," Sutherland spat.

He grabbed the kitchen table and pulled himself to his feet.

"Where's Ripley?"

She smiled and tilted her head towards the barn.

"Shit!"

He rubbed his head and slammed back his glass of bourbon sitting on the table before hitting yard at a sprint.

~

"Tommy?"

Despite his best effort to remain calm and strong, the word came out an emotional quiver.

"Dad."

Mark and Tommy got to their feet at the same time, but Tommy came to Mark first, wrapping his arms around him and squeezing him hard.

"I love you, Dad."

"I know, son."

"Dad—"

"I know."

Sutherland burst through the door.

"Ripley, don't."

Tommy clenched his fists, facing Sutherland.

"Dale," Tommy said, a warning in his tone.

"It's okay, Tommy," Mark said. "I know. You were a kid. This isn't your fault."

"What do you think you know?" Sutherland said.

"Think I know?" Mark said. "Think?" There's no think about it."

Jackie came in the door behind Sutherland and walked over behind Mark and Tommy.

"You lied to me, you son of a bitch," Mark said. "For years."

Sutherland sputtered, then pointed at Tommy. "Not just me, Mark. Sarah too. And Tommy."

"He was a child, you asshole!" Mark turned to Tommy. "I don't fault you for this. Not one little bit."

"He's the one who's made this all difficult. This is all his fault."

"YOU!"

Mark lunged forward and punched Sutherland across the face, opening a geyser of blood over his mouth. Sutherland took it, backing away to let Mark speak.

"You fucked her! Sarah! My wife!"

Sutherland looked down at his feet.

Pointing at Tommy, Mark said through building sobs. "My son, Dale. I believed, all these years... he's yours, Dale. Your son, yours and Sarah's.

Mark turned around and looked at Tommy. Tommy was shaking to the point of convulsion, tears rushing down his face.

"Tommy—"

"I knew, Dad. After your accident, I knew. They tested me for a blood transfusion. I asked them to. Dale and Mom told me then. I was so angry, Dad. At you, at Mom, at him." Tommy rubbed his hands over his face and pulled at his hair. "But it was never your fault, Dad. I should have told you. Should have said something."

Mark wrapped his arms around his son and held him while he cried, shook with him and let him hurt.

"You were young, Tommy. This was not your burden to bear. I have no ill will towards you. Not one little bit."

Mark pulled away and wiped Tommy's face. "And it doesn't matter. None of it matters. Regardless of blood, of lies, of life, you will always be my son. No matter what. You are my son."

They embraced again, Tommy crying word into Ripley's chest that he couldn't hear. Ripley felt the door open again and Tommy lifted his head. Someone else had come in.

"Ai," Camilla said, sauntering in beside Sutherland, lit cigarette in her hand.

"Camilla, why don't you fuck off—"

"No, Sutherland," Mark said. "I'm interested in what she has to say."

"Not much," she said. She sashayed over the Mark, stopping just before her face was touching his. "Jealous, Dale is. You had his baby, and that fucking whore. He had me, but that wasn't good enough. Wasn't satisfied with lil ol' me." She ran a slender finger up Mark's belly, then over the scar across his face. "He thought he could be you, have your life. Only took sewing a dead perp up with some explosive..."

Everyone looked at Sutherland.

The others in the barn were saying something, some at Mark, others at Sutherland. Mark didn't look at them to see what they were saying. He was focused on Sutherlands face.

"Dale?"

The scar across Mark's face throbbed, the silence in his ears a pounding rage. Sutherland's lips moved, but not forming words, just thoughts of what his words should be; it was the formation of excuses, lies.

"It's true," Mark said.

Tears in Sutherland's eyes as he looked back and forth from Mark to Tommy, finally settling on Marks face as the tears began to flow.

"Mark, I... I'm sorry. I just..."

"You just wanted to shack up with that bitch," Camilla sneered, a smile creeping across her face as she watched Sutherland stumbling.

Mark felt like he had been punched in the gut. The light waned, faces going and in and out of focus as he steadies himself on the wall, controlling his breathing to stop from passing out.

"I can't believe this," he said.

Realization dawned again, another ugly truth.

"You," Mark growled, looking back up at Sutherland.

Sutherland waited, Mark gathered his thoughts.

The boy in the tube, the box with the confetti. Sarah. Judd.

"You," Mark said, his voice rising to a yell. "You killed them! All of them!"

"Mark," Sutherland said, his eyes manic, leaping from face to face.

"You did it! All of this! And you tried to frame him?" Mark looked at Tommy, who was staring at Sutherland, his face red with anger. "You realized," Mark continued, "that he would in no way, ever be your son."

Mark looked at Tommy and took his hand.

"You are my son. Always."

Tommy cried and embraced his father, and the two held each other.

"No," Sutherland said. "He—"

He never finished the sentence. Mark felt the noise deep in his bones, the smell of gunpowder burning the insides of his nostrils.

Dale Sutherland wavered on his feet, his words halted in a gaping mouth as crimson spread across the front of his shirt. His hands found the exit wound on his belly. His eyes closed, and he nodded his head.

"Mark."

Only able to take one step before he dropped, Sutherland collapsed against the wall, sliding down and settling in the spot of his final breath. Camilla stood, gun in hand, looking quite pleased with herself.

"Long time coming, you prick."

She tossed the gun on the ground at Sutherland's feet before looking Mark in the eye, giving him a single nod, and leaving the barn.

Tommy was white as a ghost, looking at Sutherland, and Jackie Fields stood back, crying as she radioed the station.

"Tommy," Mark said, taking his hand. "What's downstairs?"

Eyes, blue and brown, grey and hazel, floated in jars, fixed in vacant wonder. Light poured from the industrial bulbs above, coating the eyes in glistening tears. But the eyes were not sad. They were nothing, just orbs of fibrous tissue, empty and unfeeling. In them, Ripley imagine the terror of their last moments. Next to the eyes were jars of bones. Tiny, delicate bones.

"What are you thinking?" Field's asked.

"I'm thinking that some days—most days—I hate the world."

Ripley poked a jar as if to challenge its reality. It really was there. Unfortunately. The room was as barren as the eyes, devoid of warmth, decency, and beauty. A dental chair, top of the line medical equipment, and lights.

Horrible lights, benign on their own, but menacing in relation to the product of their illumination.

On the counter below the jars of eyes were several trays. Mark walked over and put his nose down to one of the trays.

They are like little shells. Souvenirs from a day at the beach or some exotic location.

But they weren't shells, and their origin was not tropical nor exotic. They were bones. Tiny bones, some still stained with the signature of their owner's blood. Bones so small, so wispy and delicate they could have come from the bodies of baby birds. But he knew.

Jackie touched Mark's arm, said something he didn't see.

Mark should have walked away, waited for the CSI's and detectives to take over, but he was curious. Morbidly so. He hated himself for it, but he yearned to crawl inside Sutherland's mind and find out what preceded this particular brand of lunacy.

I was a good jaunt from the front door of the demon's lair. I took long strides, hoping to minimize the time the journey would consume and therefore my time at that horror show, but my surroundings contradicted my hustling fear. Children, playing and laughing, oblivious to the flurry of law enforcement buzzing around like locusts. Beautiful young hearts, dancing, singing. I couldn't bear to watch them lest my stomach claw its way up into my throat. The birds sang in rhythm with my footfalls, peaceful and melodic, attempting to carry my heavy feet on the wings of their song. *Damn this place, this illusion of the devil.* Evil wears this utopia of contentment and peace like a mask.

Camilla was seated on a floral chesterfield, sipping on a tea of sweet chamomile or peppermint or some other delicate flavour that had no business passing her lips. Mark wanted to swat it out of her hands and penetrate her ivory flesh with the shards. Instead, he took his place across from her.

"Camille," he said, clenching his fists.

"Mark," she said, looking at me over her long lashes.

"You knew. All along."

"I did."

She took a sip of her tea. Mark hoped that she'd choke on it.

"All this, just to get at me?"

"For him, yes."

"And you?"

Another sip.

"You don't understand, do you?"

"I don't, no. Will you explain?"

"Why? Will it change your mind?"

"Change my mind? In regard to what? His guilt? Yours? Not likely."

"The world's sickness. The solution."

What?

"Do you tire of it, Detective?"

"Tire of what?"

"The senseless violence. The hate. I can't sit by and condone it any longer. No one should. Day after day, death after death, hate upon hate, force fed to us until our minds are bloated and splitting at the seams, so completely satiated with negativity that we vomit." She took a sip of her tea, her slender hands shaking with rage. "We purge the overindulged meals of our sensory inundation, the excess manifesting itself in the form of more hate, more violence. The cycle is eternal."

Bodies floated in Mark's mind, the young man suspended in the tube, that suffering man in the hospital. Kind old Judd, gouged, his last moments that of torment and terror.

"There is a darkness in all of us, sure," she continued. "But it's how that darkness grows, how it is *fed* that is destroying us as a species."

"Once upon a time, after I first received my medical degree, I wondered what it would be like to never know," she mused. "To never know the lies and hate we are force-fed by the media, by our families, by our neighbours, by the men who take us and use us and ruin us. To never know the anger and hate that unites the lost and lonely in the worst way possible."

Balls bounced, rolling from tiny, fumbling palms.

"Every day we are assaulted with campaigns *against* rather than *for*. We need to be unified by more than our disdain, but it's easier to be angry, especially when others are. Hate is a vivid emotion and intoxicating when one craves exhilaration."

Laughter. Hugs. Smiles. Ringlets bouncing in the gentle breeze.

"The sludge of the world has been forced into us through our fingertips by social media, and through the voices of biased media. But what would it be like to never see it?"

Those eyes in the jars, along with the hammer, anvil, and stirrup bones from his ears. Conducted as a standard procedure akin to the removal of a foreskin would be, the eyes and the ear bones had been excised from the victims in an attempt to contain their senses, prevent interaction and social poison. Camilla wanted to throw a wrench in the social devolution of our species.

"Dale," Mark said, piecing it together. "He saw your madness when he was fucking you and used it to frame my Tommy."

Her voice was light and airy. Proud. "There are ways, Mark. The deaf and blind can be taught, to read, cook, to function. Life would be about functionality and primal relations. Beautiful and savage. It's all about having the right teacher."

Mark stared at her, playing through the evidence in his mind: the mutilations, the notes, the bone…

"I mean," Camilla continued, "Anne Sullivan did it, didn't she?"

Camilla laughed. Mark couldn't hear it, but the noise still pieced his brain, a sharp blade.

"To never know is better, don't you think?" Camilla asked.

In this world? It's better not to think.

"DON'T THINK ABOUT IT TOO MUCH, MARK," JACKIE SAID, holding his hand across the center console of the Fairlane. "Just sit back and let them do their job. This is no longer your mess."

Red and blue lights flashed off the surrounding trees from the herd of police cars gathered around the barn. Police and CSI scurried around like ants, each with a task to do. Photographs were taken, evidence collected, and Camilla was being led to the back of her cruiser, hands behind her back. Mark, Tommy, and Jackie had answered a string of questions, but Captain Sloan had let them go, encouraging them to get some rest. They would need to come in tomorrow and make official statements, but they were free to go.

Tommy touched Mark's shoulder, and Mark turned around to face him.

"Dad, I love you."

Putting his hand on Tommy's, he nodded, unable to speak.

"Once this is all said and done, I might need to go away for a while."

"Rehab?" Mark said, his voice breaking.

"Yeah."

"I'll help you set it up, son. I'll be with you the whole way."

"You always have been, Dad."

Mark smiled and face forward, giving the well orchestrated law process a final glance before firing up the Fairlane. He pulled a u turn and slowly crept down the drive, leaving death and destruction behind and heading towards peace. Finally.

Never once did Ripley notice the absence of the maroon Crown Victoria...

"Right mess that was," Camilla said, sipping on her tea.

After an exhausting half year of investigations, including having their house and life torn to bits by investigators, things were finally beginning to settle. They didn't have a bit of evidence to implicate Camilla in anything. Either of them.

"That asshole Sutherland was good for something, I guess," she said. "He sure knew how to clean up a mess and hide evidence."

He glared at her. "Careful. That asshole was my father. And he loved you."

She snorted. "Not as much as he loved *her*."

"I took care of that harpy," he said, smirking, remembering the look of terror in Sarah's eyes as he put her on ice. He hated her, carrying his father's other son in her belly at the same time as he was in Camilla's.

"He loved you, you know," Camilla said. "Enough to frame his other son to protect you."

He nodded. He knew.

She settled back into her seat on their new porch, gazing out over her new piece of land on the outskirts of Picton. "You think we'll be ready to start up again soon?"

He looked over at the boy, who had stretched out another few inches, seemingly overnight.

He's growing up so quick.

The boy fingers were moving, clicking the knitting needles together as he completed another row. The knitting kept him calm. Camilla was so proud of the thing he had been able to teach the boy in such a short period of time, especially considering the only senses he had left were smell and touch.

"Yes," he said, looking in pride at his creation. "I think we'll be safe to start up again.

Anton Sutherland stood up and leaned again the railing of the patio, looking over their new farm. A large piece of land framed by Canola fields and a pasture complete with a few horses.

And a brand new red barn, the lab of creation to save the world.

GERRY MAZER is a lifelong lover of reading, writing, music, and fantastic worlds. Born in Lloydminister, Alberta, Gerry is many things: a musician, a writer, a painter, a teacher, a principal, a school district superintendent, an alderman, deputy mayor, and a retiree. Above all, he has been a wonderful husband and father, and an incredible inspiration to anyone who's known him.

ABOUT THE AUTHOR

JAE MAZER is a Canadian who was born in Victoria, British Columbia, and grew up in the prairies of Northern Alberta. After spending the majority of her life in the Great White North, she migrated south to Texas. Now she enjoys life as a mom, a wine drinker, a master of sarcasm and dark wit, a musician, and a connoisseur and creator of horror, science fiction, and fantasy. Many moons ago, a rampant love of reading led her to believe she could weave a good tale herself, and now she is an award winning author with eight novels under her belt, as well as stories published in various anthologies.

Pretty Bitchin'